PHYLLIS BOHONIS

Sarah Eisenboch

A 73 WINDSOR NOVEL

3rd Season Publications
www.3rdseason.ca

Sarah Eisenboch
© 2022, Phyllis Bohonis

All characters appearing in this work are fictitious. Any resemblance to real persons, living or dead, is purely coincidental.

Disclaimer: The locations mentioned in my novel as providing food and shelter to the city's homeless and less fortunate are completely fictitious and have no affiliation whatsoever to any of the fine shelters and soup kitchens in the City of Ottawa nor the hard-working coordinators, volunteers and donors who keep them operating. I sought to be as generic as possible in my portrayal of their functions while attempting to maintain the plausibility of the story and the fictional events within.

No part of this book may be reproduced or transmitted in any form or by any means, electronic or mechanical, including photocopying, recording, electronic transmission, or by any storage and retrieval system, without written permission from the author.

Cover design © 2022 Crowe Creations
Author photo © 2019 Phyllis Bohonis

3rd Season Publications
ISBN: 978-1-9994378-5-5

To all who assist in giving shelter and
sustenance to the homeless.

"If you live to be a hundred, I want to live to be a hundred minus one day, so I never have to live without you." — A.A. Milne

73 Windsor: Sarah Eisenboch

Chapter One

Sarah almost tripped over a heap of old rags outside the darkened entry of her trendy condo building. The smelly pile had not been there when she went out just an hour earlier. *I must ask security to remove it and to replace the light bulb as well.* As she reached to open one of the double doors she heard a sigh of sorts emanating from within the rags.

She jumped back with a shriek. "What the …?"

It was then she noticed frost on the rags inches below a closed eye barely visible through a fold of dirty cloth. Something or someone was breathing inside the heap. She looked around. Cars were going by on the street. Faint sounds of laughter emanated from the bistro a couple of doors down. She nudged the pile of rags with the toe of her winter boot to see if what was inside was conscious. It shifted slightly and dark eyes slowly focused on her.

"Okay, okay. I'll leave." The voice was weak and hoarse.

The pile shifted and a man slowly rose wrapped in several dirty grey blankets. Intimidated, Sarah took several steps back. He turned and shuffled away. *That poor soul is only seeking shelter in these freezing night temperatures.*

"No. Wait …"

The man didn't seem to hear. He stepped onto the road and limped quickly across the street, a torn strip of blanket trailing behind in the salt-encrusted road dirt. Sarah watched as he disappeared into an alley two buildings away.

Way to go, Sarah. That's starting the New Year off right. The first homeless person you encounter you give the boot to. She watched in vain to see if he might reappear.

A taxi pulled up to the sidewalk. A friend from the condominium slipped out and paid the driver. "It's a cold night to be standing around outside, Sarah. Are you waiting for someone?"

"No, Stella. I just frightened a street person away and I was waiting to see if he might return."

"Just let security know and they'll keep an eye out for him. I feel sorry for anyone out on the street on a night like this. It's got to be at least minus thirty."

"I know. I feel badly that I didn't at least offer to buy him a bowl of hot soup from the bistro."

"They may not have let him in anyway. If it's the same guy, he was here a couple of nights ago too. One of my neighbours saw him hanging around."

"Hopefully, he's gone to a shelter."

"Sarah, you worry about everyone. You can't feed and house every homeless person that walks the streets at night. Come on let's go in. Join me for a coffee upstairs?"

The feeling of self-disgust stayed with Sarah even as she got into bed after a cup of decaf coffee and one of Stella's delicious homemade cinnamon buns. The eyes that had stared back at her a couple of hours earlier continued to haunt her. With guilt she slid between her nice warm blankets and reached for the remote that turned off the gas fireplace in the corner of her comfy bedroom.

Chapter Two

Short of time, Sarah watched the local morning news only briefly for word of any deaths on the streets of Ottawa the night before. It was her turn to host the bridge game today and she still had to prepare lunch and baking. Her group of friends, all condo owners in her building and all in their sixties, played every second week taking turns hosting. She needed their laughter and gossip today as she had not slept well the night before. She had been plagued by visions of that one visible eye closing forever in the bitter, record-breaking temperature of the night before.

To keep her mind off the man, she busied herself with her preparations. Her friends always enjoyed her fancy cheesecakes and continuously praised her gourmet baking. They had no way of knowing that she had cooked and baked for her boss's wife's fancy parties back in the day when she had to earn a dollar any way she could. Sometimes she had helped serve the meals too, trying to provide a living for her and her little girl. The woman had been generous knowing Sarah was trying to keep herself and Emily away from welfare. She smiled as she thought that today she could well afford to hire a caterer to make the bridge party refreshments instead of doing it herself, but she enjoyed the creativity of baking fancy goodies. Her thoughts were interrupted by the ringing of the phone.

"I'm glad we live in the same building, otherwise I'd be calling with my regrets for this afternoon." Stella was filling in for

Olivia Kovacs, a regular in the group, who was vacationing in Florida for the month of January.

"That cold, huh?"

"They're warning people not to go out unless it's absolutely necessary. The vehicle exhaust is so bad, you can't even see across the street. Olivia is smart to head to warmer temps this time of year. Why aren't you there, by the way?"

"I was asked to organize and host the fundraiser for the hospital this year. A snowflake gala, as its name suggests, must be held in the winter months and December is always too busy to get people out. So we schedule it for early February and while the work starts in the fall, the brunt of all the arrangements takes place in January. I might go south for a month or so after the event. Why don't you plan on going down with me?"

"I'll give it some thought. I'm just calling to let you know that I have a delivery coming this morning from the grocery store. If there's anything you need, there's still time to add it.

"Thanks, I'd love some fresh whipping cream for the apricot cheesecake."

"Apricot. Hmm, don't think I've had that one before. You always have the best bridge lunch, Sarah. Are you sure you weren't a world-renowned cook in a previous life?" Stella laughed then cut the connection.

Sarah pondered the compliment and again thought of her humble beginnings. One thought led to another and she ended up wondering what or if that homeless person was eating today. A quick look out her dining room window made her shudder with relief that she didn't have to go out into the deep freeze that had settled over Ottawa. The bright sun did nothing to warm the frigid temperature. When she went downstairs later to check her mailbox, she couldn't help opening the front door of the building and looking about the sheltered outside area. She didn't really expect to see a heap of rags but something was making her wish she would. It would mean a chance to ease her guilt over the unkind way she had treated that poor man. The way he had looked at her was not with hatred, pleading, or anything distinguishable so why was she so bothered by him? He hadn't even asked for anything.

❣ ❣ ❣

"Have any of you seen that street person that's been hanging around?" Helen Mercier was sorting her playing cards as she spoke. "I noticed him a couple of nights ago. He just sits near doorways and doesn't really bother anyone for money or anything but it gives me the creeps that he's hanging around this particular neighbourhood — like he's waiting for someone."

When Sarah didn't speak up, Stella said, "It's probably the guy Sarah chased off last night."

"You chased him off?" Helen sounded surprised. "I'm surprised you didn't offer him your coat at the very least or offer him a hot meal and a warm bed for the night. You're always so generous."

Sarah laid her cards face down. "I didn't really chase him off. I thought it was just a heap of old blankets someone had tossed there. I nudged it with my foot and was surprised to see a person get up. He looked at me and just scurried off before I could stop him." Her eyes started watering.

Stella placed her hand on her friend's arm. "I didn't mean it to sound like you were being mean, I'm sorry it came out that way. We all know how kind you are to everyone, needy or not."

"I didn't sleep well last night worrying about him being out there in this deadly cold. What an unfeeling, selfish bitch he must have thought me."

"Now, Sarah, I'm sure he didn't think that at all. He's probably used to people wanting him to move on. He might have figured it was time to look for a shelter for the night anyway and when you nudged him, it moved him to action. You probably saved his life by urging him to move on. He would have surely frozen to death on our doorstep if he had stayed." Margaret Ingram, Sarah's closest friend in the group, tried to come to her defence.

"Look at us. The nice homes we have, our fireplaces keeping us cozy and warm, and look at the rich food we're eating — for snacks, for heaven's sake, not even for sustenance. Why, we don't even have to go out for our groceries. They're delivered to our door all fresh and ready to cook." The tears she had been fighting now brimmed and slowly made their way past her mascara and down her carefully blushed cheeks. "Last night I was tested and failed miserably. I let a cold, hungry man run off without offering so much as my scarf to him. Then I came upstairs and climbed into my nice warm bed after having hot coffee and warm buns at Stella's.

"Where did that man go? To another doorway? To a shelter where, if he was lucky, he may have been allowed to sleep on the floor? Did he even eat yesterday? Is he alive today?" She hastily stood and left the table.

Helen looked sadly at the others around the table. "I am so sorry I brought this up. I, in my own selfish way, saw just another homeless man when he was sitting out there the other night. I offered him some money but he ignored me. I didn't even bother to see if he was breathing, I just assumed he didn't want it or was sleeping. Sarah, on the other hand, sees someone who hasn't been as blessed as we are and feels guilty about having more than him. I'm sure she wishes she had invited him in for a hot meal and a good night's sleep by the fireplace."

She stood. "I'm sorry for putting a damper on our card game." Then went to find Sarah.

Sarah was in her ensuite dabbing cold water on her face. She saw Helen in the mirror and tried to make light of the situation. "My God, look at me. If that man saw me here and now, I'm sure he would run off again only this time in fear."

Helen took her arm and urged her toward the door. "Come on. We'll all have some of that expensive brandy you keep stored in your liquor cabinet and put this behind us. Besides, I'm ahead and I'm not going to let you do me out of finally winning a round."

Chapter Three

"So, Margaret, you and your new-found family are all still on speaking terms? No one has threatened to kill anyone yet?" Stella tried to find neutral ground to start a fresh conversation.

Margaret, recently married for the second time, had moved from her modest condo a floor below into one of the largest in the building with her new husband and his family.

"No. We're all still speaking." She laughed at the thought of Clarke's family being anything but loving. "The children are kept busy with their sports and school activities. Mitchell, our son-in-law, spends his time between chauffeuring them and at the long-term hospital where Clarke's daughter is, so we manage to keep out of each other's hair."

"How is Kirsten's therapy coming along?"

"She's determined to walk again so she's doing everything she's told without complaint and then some. They think by late spring, she may be able to come home." Margaret's new stepdaughter, Kirsten, had been in a horrific accident in South America followed by a long period of recovery in a Peruvian hospital before finally being transported to an Ottawa hospital. Her husband had been reported missing after the same accident and it was months before he was found alive and brought back to Canada. "Clarke is so relieved by her progress. Did I tell you we're going to Hawaii for two weeks in March?"

Helen perked up at that. "Please let Clarke's family know that Gerald and I can help with the kids. We pseudo-grandparents will enjoy filling in while you and Clarke are away."

The conversation and the card game continued until late afternoon when Sarah brought out the cheesecake topped with freshly whipped cream. No one brought up the topic of rich food again nor did they mention how well Sarah baked but they each took a piece of the rich cake home with them.

After Sarah closed the door behind them, she poured another cup of tea for herself. She stood drinking her tea in front of her twelfth-floor window and tried to figure out how to find the man she had turned away from the door the night before. *And if you find him, what are you going to do about him?*

♥ ♥ ♥

That evening, the temperature didn't drop as much as it had the night before but the snow started falling. And falling. And falling.

After the evening news, Sarah dug a hooded parka from her closet, donned a toque and wool-lined leather gloves and warm winter boots. She took the elevator down to the main floor, narrowly missing Helen and Gerald who stepped into the second elevator as she exited hers. The security person ensconced in his little office facing the foyer cautioned her about going out on such a night but she reassured him she was only going down the street.

The wind and snow caught her full force in the face as she went out the door. The small, protected entrance area was already covered in a snow drift circling around one of the stone pillars that should have acted as a wind block. A shovel leaned against the wall and there was evidence that someone had recently made an attempt to clear the snow from in front of the double doorway. There was no heap of old blankets visible.

Sarah looked both ways and decided to cross the street and

peek down the alleyway the man had scurried into the night before. It was dark and blocked with snow piled from the neighbouring business owners pushing the powdery stuff into it from in front of their doors. She shone her penlight down the narrow passage but the light didn't carry very far. No one seemed to be in the street. Only those who absolutely had to, would venture outdoors tonight. She checked a few doorways up and down her street to no avail then attempted to turn the corner but the wind caught her and she had to keep her head down to avoid the blowing snow. It would be futile to comb the neighbourhood. All she could do was hope and pray that all the homeless had found shelter indoors.

That night she dreamt of a multitude of one-eyed people closing in on her in a dark alley. But one stayed in the background, not moving — only staring.

Chapter Four

The cold weather continued into the second week of January. The strong winds continued but did manage to move the snowy conditions into Quebec and the Maritimes, restoring Ottawa to bright sunshine. Sarah chose to take taxis to her many meetings in preparation for the gala fundraiser. They were mostly at the National Arts Centre which, in warmer weather, would have been within walking distance of her condo.

She had just returned to her own apartment after enjoying lunch with Margaret and Clarke at their place, when her cell phone rang. It was Stella.

"I'm downstairs, and Frank, the day security, told me that the night security person had to call an ambulance to take a street person to the hospital last night. Andy, the night guy, had gone outside for a smoke shortly after ten o'clock and the man was bundled up outside the door. He asked him to leave but got no response. When he tried to lift the man to his feet, the guy keeled over and Andy couldn't get any reaction from him."

"Oh, no. The poor man. Do either Frank or Andy know if the man is okay?"

"No. Once the ambulance left, Andy logged the incident but of course it's not his place to follow up on it."

"I wonder … I'll see what I can find out. Thanks for letting me know, Stella."

"Sarah, don't go doing anything silly …" She was talking to dead air.

Sarah looked up the phone number for the Ottawa General. After attempts to get information from both the General and Civic campuses of the Ottawa hospital, she knew nothing more. Andy wouldn't be on duty again until four o'clock, still two hours away. After pacing the floor for half an hour, she decided to inquire in person and within fifteen minutes she left the parking garage.

No one could or would give her any information. She tried pretending she was looking for a relative but without being able to give them a name she was met with apologies and explanations of patient privacy. A nurse, sensing her need for an answer, touched her arm as Sarah turned to leave. "Ma'am, an ambulance did arrive with a dishevelled looking man late last night but the patient refused treatment and hurried out on his own. The young man was upright and walking, that's all I can tell you."

"Young man? How young?"

"I'd guess mid-twenties."

"Did you notice his eyes? Were they dark?"

"I'm sorry. I've already told you more than I should have."

She marched out of the hospital in frustration. Once inside her car she gave the steering wheel a pounding and with tears in her eyes exited the parking lot. She was sure the man she had turned away was much older than that. Maybe it wasn't even the same person. Still … it was a person, a man needing shelter. There was nothing to do but go home.

At four o'clock sharp, she was downstairs only to learn that it was Andy's night off. The six o'clock news brought no information about anyone dying from the cold on the Ottawa streets the night before. All she could do was pray he had found a warm bed.

♥ ♥ ♥

The next few weeks she was kept busy with meetings called by various boards on which she sat. At the next bridge game, she brought up the subject of the street man, but no one had any more information than she did and no one had seen him again. Andy didn't know any more than he had reported to Frank. The cold snap had come to an end and she hoped that the man had not suffered any more cold nights in *any* doorway of *any* building. She could not help wondering what his story was though.

February was approaching and everything was falling into place for the gala. It was time to make flight reservations for her trip to Florida. Stella had decided not to go with her. She felt she shouldn't leave her employment agency for seniors when so many who had lost temporary jobs before Christmas would be looking for springtime employment. It was a business that Helen Mercier had started while she was still Helen Whittaker. It had proved so successful that Stella bought it when Helen married Gerald Mercier a couple of years earlier.

Sarah knew that Olivia would be back any day now having been in Florida for two months. A lot of the condominiums in Sarah's building down there were owned or rented by Canadians who returned year after year, so she wouldn't be lonely down there. She always felt a little guilty about having a three-bedroom condo and not sharing it with friends who might like to spend a few weeks in the hot sun. She, like a lot of owners, rented their units out when not using them, but lately Sarah had been thinking of cancelling her contract with the rental agency. It might be nice for it to be at her disposal on a moment's notice if the whim to head south for a week or two seized her.

A few phone calls took care of all the loose ends for the big party. The caterers were set to go. The seating arrangements for the dignitaries were complete. The Master of Ceremonies was confirmed as were the news media and entertainment. The auctioneer was well-known and familiar with the items being auctioned. All that was left for Sarah to do was a final fitting for her dress that had been designed and sewn by her own favourite local designer. She didn't have an escort for the evening but never felt the need for one. When she was hostess for these events, she wanted to be able to free-wheel rather than be tied to the arm of a man who might feel neglected if she got called to take care of any unforeseen emergencies.

She was being joined, however, by her son. He would be attending representing his own investment firm. He was flying in from his home in Montreal the morning of the event and meeting with several investors in the afternoon. His plans were to stay the night with his mother then leave for Vancouver in the morning.

Gordon's life was so busy that Sarah always treasured the few hours they could spend together. Montreal was less than an hour by air from Ottawa and less than two by car but it may as well have been on the other side of the world for how often they actually saw each other. In any event, it was a gazillion times more often than she saw her daughter, Emily, who lived in Toronto.

Chapter Five

"I thought Olivia was going to be back in time to go to this thing." Gordon called from the guest bedroom after arriving from his meetings with only time to shower, shave and change into his tuxedo.

"I was hoping she would but she got talked into going with friends to Veradero for a few days. She won't be back until next week."

"Isn't that kind of rude, backing out on you like that?"

"No, she's not rude. Olivia feels sorry for me and sometimes agrees without thinking to do things with me that her heart isn't really into. I learned long ago not to take it personally when she finds reasons to cancel. If you weren't a willing escort, she would have come back."

"The two of you are good friends, why can't she just say no without hurting your feelings?"

"It's my fault. I should know better than to ask her. She doesn't like going to events like this and having to mix with people she's not familiar with."

"A good-looking woman like her? She can't be self-conscious. She keeps herself in good shape. Always looks like a fox. Why would she not want to go out and be seen?"

"Beats me. There are any number of men who are disappointed when she doesn't show."

"Hmm. Strange. She's certainly not shy."

"Oh well. Olivia is Olivia and she's not going to change. Are you about ready to roll?"

"I just need help putting these cufflinks in. I hate French cuffs on shirts. Whoever invented them was a sadist."

"Whoever invented them was probably the same person that invented spike heels."

"You've got the ankles for them, Mom. You look fantastic." He kissed her cheek and held her coat for her.

♥ ♥ ♥

The evening went by without too many incidents. Any that happened went unnoticed. They raised a record amount of money with the auction, and the entertainment — an up-and-coming Latin band — was well-received. It was almost midnight when Sarah and Gordon were able to leave the banquet room. Gordon was happy having made a couple of important business connections and Sarah was happy that the food, entertainment and auction were a success.

The taxi dropped them off in front of Sarah's condominium and Andy greeted them as they came in the door. "Mrs. Eisenboch, there was a dishevelled looking guy out front for a short while tonight. He just hung around, walked back and forth a few times, then left. He seems strong enough. I don't think he suffered any health problems. Probably just exposure or hypothermia."

"Did you talk to him?"

"No. Didn't want to encourage him. The other people here want me to discourage the street bums from hanging around our building."

Sarah frowned at his terminology. "You're sure it was the same man?"

"A street guy is a street guy. I can't remember exactly what they all look like."

"Andy, do me a favour and ring me if you see him out front again?"

"Mrs. Eisenboch, I don't think you should be talking to guys like him."

"I will decide who I should and shouldn't talk to, young man. Just let me know if he reappears." Sarah walked through the foyer with Gordon close behind.

"What was that all about, Mother?"

"Last month there was a man out front. He didn't seem well, and I unintentionally sent him on his way on an extremely cold night without even offering him the means for a hot meal. I've been feeling guilty ever since."

"I know how kind you are to people but you can't help every single derelict in the world. If you miss one or two along the way, you can't beat yourself up over it. He probably went to a shelter where he had a warm bed and a hot meal."

"I suppose. There was just something about him that … Well, it doesn't matter now. He's probably moved on to another neighbourhood. Hopefully, one with people who are little more generous. If what Andy says is true, that poor, unfortunate man, and others like him, are not welcome around here."

♥ ♥ ♥

They watched a replay of the late news together then Gordon, scheduled to take an early flight in the morning, went off to bed promising not to wake her. Sarah undressed and lay awake in bed thinking about the man who had returned to the street that night. Was there something or someone that was attracting him to this particular street? To this particular building? If she stared hard enough she could imagine his face on the ceiling. *What is your story?* She finally fell asleep after turning onto her side.

She was awake and had hot coffee waiting for her son by the time he was out of the shower.

"Are you sure you don't want me to drive you to the airport, darling?"

"There's no need. Thanks anyway. I've already called for a driver and he'll be downstairs in ten minutes." He took the steaming coffee mug she handed him.

"How long will you be in Vancouver?"

"Probably three days. I have two days of business meetings then I'm meeting some friends for a day of skiing. Can't go to British Columbia and not ski." He quickly swallowed some coffee, bussed her cheek and picked up his bag.

She followed him to the door where, with a look of concern, he cautioned, "Mom, don't let the fact that you innocently turned away a street person get to you. You know he's still around which means he's alive and healthy. Reasonably healthy anyway. You've helped enough people that I don't think God is going to close the door on you because you let one get away. In fact, I would be quite surprised if you haven't already made a generous donation to one of the shelters hoping to make it up to him."

The blush that came to her cheeks told him he was right.

"Go to Florida and enjoy your time with your friends down there."

She smiled. "I've already got my flight booked."

Chapter Six

The Florida sun did little to warm the chill Sarah had been experiencing since that early January night. The golf course and dinners with friends didn't give her any respite either. Try as she might to shake it off, she could not get rid of the foreboding she felt.

The doorbell interrupted her thoughts. The handsome grey-haired man who smiled at her when she opened the door always made her day a little brighter. "Jake, come in. When did you get here?"

"This morning. I had hoped to be here last night, but I got a late start out of Chicago on Tuesday and stayed overnight in Louisville then I had to spend last night in Gainesville. This old body just can't sit in the car for thirteen hours straight anymore."

Jakub Tatarek, a retired engineer from rural Chicago, had been renting a condo in the building for about the same number of years as Sarah. His usual stay was eight weeks from early February until late March. This year, he was a couple of weeks late because of a friend's illness and subsequent death. He and Sarah had become close friends and always enjoyed their time together.

"I'll mix you a drink. Make yourself comfortable on the balcony."

For a big man, his gait was fluid and light. He was dressed for the heat in a pair of khaki shorts, golf shirt and sandals and sank smoothly onto one of the chaises in the shade of the overhang. When Sarah handed him a cool iced tea, he took her hand in his and placed a kiss on the back of it.

"How is Tom's wife doing?" Sarah sat in the chair beside him.

"She's fine. She said to thank you for the flowers you sent." Jake set his glass down and turned to look at Sarah. "You don't look like you've been getting much sun."

"I've been on the golf course but I've mostly been catching up on my favourite author's latest book. I had a hectic month in January preparing for last week's gala so I'm enjoying some downtime."

"Have you seen Gert and Steve?"

"No. Like I said, I've mostly been keeping to myself."

He gave her a long stare. "You aren't ill or anything, I hope."

She knew it wouldn't be long before he picked up on her melancholy. He was usually able to read her moods. Trying to nip it in the bud, she replied. "I'm absolutely fine. Winter in Ottawa was exceptionally cold this year and I didn't get away as early as I usually do. I guess it's taking me a little longer to acclimate myself to the heat."

"How was your gala?"

"It was a huge success. People are so generous. We increased our total funds-raised by fifteen per cent this year."

"Now you can relax and enjoy your downtime. Maybe we can get in some deep-sea fishing. I have to finish unpacking and pick up a few things for the fridge. Can we have an early supper out somewhere?"

"We could. However, you've been on the road for two days and eating in fast food places along the way most likely. Why don't you let me fix you something nourishing, then maybe we can go for a walk?"

"What are you implying? Fried chicken, burgers and fries aren't nourishing?"

"Oh, there are probably some vitamins, minerals and protein in there somewhere but I think it's time you had food that's steamed or fresh. Come back around 4:30 or 5:00 and we'll have a nice dinner and watch some golf. I think the PGA tournament is in Hawaii this week."

"Have you ever been to Hawaii, Sarah?"

"No. That's one place, I've always wanted to visit and never have. Some of my friends are going next month."

"I was there many years ago. Waikiki. I'll bet it's a lot different now." He stood to leave. "Why don't we make plans to go there in the fall?"

Sarah hesitated. She and Jake had been close, very close, but the thought of actually travelling together and sharing a hotel room like a couple was something she had never pictured the two of them doing. Their relationship had always been an easy, comfortable one rather than a romantic one. He sensed her hesitation.

"We can rent a two-bedroom beach cottage or condo. That way we're together but separate."

"Jake, I …"

He squeezed her shoulders when she stood up. "Sarah, you and I are too close not to have a sense about each other's feelings. I know we have a special friendship and I wouldn't want to make you uncomfortable, but I can't think of a travel companion with whom I would have more fun. We enjoy the same things. There's plenty of time to think about it."

He kissed her warmly but briefly on the mouth and waited for her to smile. She blushed, nodded and put a hand on one of his. "I guess I'm afraid that too much togetherness might spoil your opinion of me. So far, I've been able to fool you into believing I'm even-tempered and good-natured. I don't want to lose that."

She kissed him back then turned him in the direction of the door. "Now, go do your errands and get your clothes unpacked. I'll fix some food for us, we'll watch some golf and after the sun goes down, we'll take that walk on the beach."

Jake always managed to take her breath away. She leaned against the closed door. He reminded Sarah so much of her last husband, both in nature and physical appearance. The kindness and easy manner were such a part of both men. It was what she had loved about Harry and what had oiled the wheels driving her to such a close and trusting friendship with Jake. They would never be more than friends, well, *maybe* travel companions. Sarah had no desire to marry again. She liked the freedom that a single life gave her. After three husbands, she didn't want to be encumbered with another — no matter how nice he was. Jake had always seemed satisfied with their friendship as well. The topic of anything more permanent had never come up. Theirs was a Florida relationship: golfing, fishing, walking, dining. They enjoyed all the same things and were completely comfortable with occasional lapses in conversation. Away from Ottawa, he was her best friend. *Please don't spoil it, Jake!*

♥ ♥ ♥

A few hours later, the doorbell rang. Jake was rested and ready to eat. Sarah motioned him to a buffet of cold smoked fish and various sliced and diced veggies with some cottage cheese and fresh baked biscuits. They watched the evening news and a few early holes of the PGA golf tournament from Hawaii. The sun was low in the sky when Jake patted her thigh and suggested they go for a walk to get some ice cream.

The days seemed brighter, the water bluer, and the white clouds puffier when Jake was around.

Chapter Seven

A week or so later, Sarah was closing the door on her way out when her phone rang. She slipped back inside and dug her phone out of her bag.

"Hi, Mom. Whatcha up to?"

"Gordon, how nice to hear your voice. I was on my way out the door to meet friends for a round of golf."

"Nice day for golf down there?"

"It sure is. Seventy-six degrees with nice intermittent clouds."

"We have a snowstorm *again*. Third time this month."

Sarah laughed. "Well, darling, you may just have to jump on a plane and get your butt down here for a week or so."

"Actually, that's what I'm calling about. I talked to Sandra and she's allowing Gracie to spend a week with me. If we aren't infringing on any plans you may have, I was hoping I might bring her down for little visit."

"That's wonderful, Gordon. It will be fun to have my granddaughter here. You too, if absolutely necessary." She smiled. "Stay for as long as you can. When are you planning on coming?"

"I was thinking I'd drive down to New York sometime today and pick her up for a flight out maybe tomorrow. I'll have to see what I can arrange and get back to you later. Is that okay?"

"Of course. Let me know and I'll pick you up at the airport."

"No need. I'll rent a car and drive over. I'm hoping we can be there by noon or so, but I'll let you know. Go enjoy your golf and we'll see you tomorrow."

Sarah considered cancelling the golf. The opportunities to spend time with her granddaughter were few and far between. Sandra, Gordon's ex-wife, was extremely stingy about the time Sarah was allowed to spend with their child. She felt she should bake and checked her freezer for food suitable to please a pre-teen appetite. She glanced toward the window and saw a white cloud shaped like a beckoning finger and knew the golf course was calling her. There was ample time to shop and bake between now and noon tomorrow.

The day was hotter than she had anticipated and the women decided nine holes of golf were enough. They ate a light lunch in the clubhouse then Sarah left to go home and prepare for her family's arrival.

She called Jake to tell him the good news about her visitors and received an invitation to go for pizza. The poor man hadn't had any junk food in over a week and his body was letting him know that it was time. Of course, properly chosen, pizzas didn't necessarily fit the junk food category but Jake's choice of toppings would put it over the top. She accepted his invitation with the condition they would stop at a supermarket on the way home.

"You are so lucky to have your family close enough to visit. With Charlotte living half way around the world in Australia, I get to see her and my grandkids maybe every second year."

"I can't imagine what that must be like. I feel sorry for myself when Gracie's mother won't let her come to Canada more often than two or three times a year. Gordon gets to see her more often but only on weekends in New York. I'm blessed that he brings her to see me during a couple of the Canadian visits. Emily is another matter, but I've learned not to push my daughter when it comes to her or my grandsons. Those boys are old enough to see me on their own if they chose to. Chris always said that he wanted to go to university away from Toronto so I had hoped he might come to Ottawa but he chose London."

Sarah felt the conversation taking a downward slant and wasn't about to let the negatives of either hers or Jake's grandparenting, or lack thereof, ruin the happiness of her pending company. She reached across the table and placed her hand on top of his. "There's nothing stopping you from taking a trip to Australia for a visit with your grandchildren.

"If you're finished your pizza, I have some shopping to do." She eyed the half slice of double cheese, double pepperoni pizza left on his plate. "Do you want to take that home for a midnight snack?"

"Hell no. I know exactly where to draw the line between satisfying a craving and courting a heart attack. Five and a half slices is exactly where I stop." He winked at the waiter who came to take their plates away. "A man's gotta keep in fighting shape, ain't that right, son?"

"Yes, sir. It takes a real man to know when to push away from the table." He surprised Sarah with his quick comeback. However, when the young man bid Jake goodbye by name, she realized her "real man" must be a frequent customer.

Sarah stroked off the items on her list as Jake pushed the cart and watched it fill. "How big is this twelve-year-old?"

"You remember her, Jake. She's a wee spit of a thing, just like her mother. Why do you ask?"

"I thought she must have grown into the size of a line-backer if she's gonna eat this much food."

Sarah slapped his shoulder. "Her father has a healthy appetite and I would rather have too much than too little."

"Spoken like a true grandmother. I'll bet you're going home to bake ten dozen cookies, a coupla pies and a layer cake. Maybe some brownies thrown in for good measure."

"Shush! You know it will be you and Gordon eating most of it."

She baked only six dozen cookies, one lemon meringue pie and two dozen chocolate cupcakes. At some point before they would leave, she planned on making Gordon's favourite: rhubarb and strawberry crumble with whipped cream. Even though cooking and baking for others had been her main source of income in the early years, she still loved it and was happy to have people around who appreciated it.

♥♥♥

Gordon and Gracie arrived shortly after noon and Sarah hoped they had brought appetites with them. The snacks on the plane certainly could not have been enough to satisfy the hunger of a healthy man and a growing pre-teen. Gracie's emotion at seeing her grandmother was almost non-existent. It hurt, but Sarah chalked it up to the girl's age, recalling that her own kids had been about that age when it was no longer cool to hug and kiss their parents.

She had remembered that Gracie had always liked her homemade mac and cheese so she had a steaming casserole on the table shortly after their arrival. Gordon dug right in, piling his plate high and spooning a portion onto his daughter's plate. The girl told her dad he had given her way too much but Sarah told her to eat only as much as she wanted. It was not an overly large portion and she thought perhaps the child was just being shy.

Gracie filled her grandmother in on her school activities. She was in a private middle school for girls, which had a good athletic program. She liked the ice hockey program and had proven to be a strong skater. Their season would be coming to an end soon and then Gracie would try out for the track team. All the while the girl talked, she pushed her food around on her plate with very little of it actually making it to her mouth. Sarah offered some freshly sliced cucumber and tomato which the girl accepted and ate with relish.

"Why don't we take a plate of cupcakes out to the balcony and watch some of the beach activity? There are usually some para-sailors putting on a show out there and there's a nice breeze for it today. Maybe later we can go down and splash around either in the pool or the ocean."

"My coach told me I have to be careful about sweets and starches, Grandma. Since I had the macaroni, I better not have any cupcakes."

Sarah was about to tell her granddaughter that she was on a holiday which allows for a little indulgence but she caught Gordon giving her a slight shake of his head behind Gracie.

Chapter Eight

After two days, it was apparent to Sarah that Gracie was barely eating enough to keep her alive and she approached Gordon about it.

"I know you're concerned, Mom, but she's only trying to drop a couple of pounds of fat and develop more muscle. The track team is very competitive and she wants desperately to make it."

"But she's not eating enough for a growing girl. Her body is developing and needs the nourishment."

"You see she eats the fresh veggies you give her and she's running on the beach."

"Yes, I see that. I'm surprised she doesn't want to tan. She wears her baggy track pants and T-shirts. I would have thought she would love to go back and show off a nice tan to her friends. She hasn't even been in the water."

"Mom, cool it. You said it yourself, her body is developing. She's getting curves she never had before and losing baby fat in other places. She's at the age where she and her friends are afraid of getting fat. Sandra told me they're getting picky about what they will and will not eat and she asked me to please not harp on it. It's just a phase and better that than eating all the junk food some kids crave."

"I suppose. I guess I'm disappointed that she's not enjoying all the old favourites of hers that I've been making."

"Just keep putting out the veggies and fruit and you'll see her eat. Let me take care of all that other good stuff you've been cooking. I'm on vacation too and I certainly am willing to indulge." He reached for another cupcake and grinned at her as he popped the whole thing in his mouth.

"Jake invited me to go with him to the club tomorrow and hit eighteen holes. Would you mind if I left Gracie in your hands for a few hours?"

"Mind? I would love it. I'll see if she'd like to go with me to get our fingernails done, maybe a pedicure while we're at it. We'll have a girls' day out."

♥♥♥

They ended up getting their hair done as well. Gracie had wanted a style that involved shaving one side of her head but, thinking of Sandra's reaction, Sarah talked her into something less extreme.

"That was so much fun, Grandma. Wait until my friends see how fancy my pedicure is. I only wish it was permanent. I hope my nails don't grow too fast. Thank you for taking me." Gracie flashed her grandmother a huge smile.

Sarah's heart skipped a beat. It was the first real sign of pleasure Gracie had shown since her arrival. It wasn't a hug but it was a genuine smile.

That evening, Jake joined them for dinner at one of the excellent seafood restaurants. Gracie had agreed saying she loved shrimp. Maybe it had just taken some bonding at a feminine spa to open up the young girl and help her feel more like family rather than a guest. Sarah kept her fingers crossed that Gracie might enjoy some of the fresh-caught Florida fare that was available at every restaurant and vendor's booth.

They rode in Gordon's SUV rental to one of the cafes on the Intracoastal Waterway. It was a great evening for eating on the outside patio. Sarah's family had only one more full day in

Clearwater before heading back to New York. As she sat in the back seat with her tiny granddaughter beside her they compared their manicures. Sarah had loaned Gracie a pair of turquoise earrings to go with the new T-shirt the girl had found at one of the markets. Gracie was fairer skinned than her dad with almost turquoise-coloured eyes. She resembled her mother in every way from her petite size to the long slender fingers and slightly turned-up nose. The only evidence of Gordon's gene in her make-up was her slightly curled hair and well-arched eyebrows.

Gracie caught her grandmother giving her the once over and responded with a smile. "Do you like my hair cut, Grandma? You don't think it's too short?"

"I think it's a beautiful haircut. The style is the perfect frame for your oval face and long neck. The stylist knew what she was doing."

"I hope my mom likes it. She might be upset that I got it cut without her."

"How can she not like it? You look so pretty."

"Mom doesn't like me doing things on my own. She always says she knows what's best for me and I sometimes make bad decisions."

Sarah's heart went out to the child. She hoped that Sandra wasn't choking Gracie's ability to think for herself. It might diminish her self-esteem at a vulnerable time in her life.

"If she doesn't approve, it won't take long to grow out. Then it was a good decision you made to not get a really drastic cut."

"Yes. I'm happy now that I didn't. I like this one." She reached for Sarah's hand and held on to it until they arrived at their destination.

They received their menus and Sarah's elation at hearing Gracie order a sugary fruit drink was quickly undone when the girl ordered a salad.

"I thought you loved seafood."

"I do but it's pretty fatty and I only like it when it's in butter sauce."

"I can't talk you into it just for one night?"

"My mother says if you give in to the small temptations you will never be able to refuse the big ones."

"Okay, I wouldn't want to go against your mother's wishes." She leaned over and stage-whispered into Gracie's ear. "But I won't peek if someone accidentally knocks a shrimp off my plate onto hers and then has to eat it so it won't be wasted."

Gracie giggled.

Sarah couldn't help feeling a little disappointed that her son didn't have some say in what his daughter did and didn't do when she was under his supervision.

In the end, Gracie did take a scant spoonful of Sarah's gelato.

They walked along the boardwalk, women in front, men behind. The temperature was always a little warmer on this side of the peninsula. Gracie admired some of the larger boats docked at the marina. So did her dad.

"Would you like to go for a ride in one, Gracie?" Jake had been watching her apparent admiration of the boats.

"I've never been in a boat, Mr. Tatarek."

That surprised even Sarah. "Not even in Montreal?"

"Nope."

Sarah raised an eyebrow at her son.

"It never entered the picture. I'm not a fisherman nor do I waterski. I don't think I even know anyone who owns a boat."

Jake spoke up. "Then we have to change this situation. Sarah, we have to take these landlubbers out fishing. If you folks don't have plans, I'll make arrangements for us to go out in the morning for a few hours."

Gracie looked quickly up at her dad. "Could we, Daddy, please?"

"Do you know how to swim?"

"A little. Mom enrolled me in swimming lessons a few years ago but I didn't like the feel of water in my ears so as soon as I learned to tread water and float on my back, she let me quit."

"We'll have to put life jackets on anyway so that's not a problem. I can call my friend right now and reserve a boat. Yes? No?"

"Please, Daddy?"

"If Grandma thinks that it's okay and she doesn't have any plans for us, then I don't see why not."

"Since it's up to me I think you better rent the boat, Jake."

"I'll find José's number."

He walked off to one side for a few minutes and returned grinning. "Little lady, you're going fishing tomorrow in a real boat, just about the size of one of these." He pointed to a row of approximate thirty-four-foot-long yachts moored along the pier.

"This is the best holiday ever." Gracie reached for her dad and gave him a big hug.

"I think it's Jake who deserves the hug."

The little girl looked at the burly older man, then shyly wrapped her arms around his waist and squeezed.

Sarah noticed the moisture in Jake's eyes as he patted the young girl's shoulder.

Chapter Nine

"The child never put on a bathing suit the whole time she was here."

"Mom, it's a phase she's going through." Gordon was waiting for his daughter to finish her run on the beach and shower before loading their luggage into the vehicle. "Sandra says that Gracie and her friends are dedicated to making the track team this spring. The try-outs are next week and it's a big plus in her school record if she's an accomplished, all-round athlete. She'll be fine."

"An accomplished athlete? She's only turning thirteen this spring. Isn't her junior or senior year in high school time enough to worry about college entrance requirements?"

"It's not the same as it used to be, Mom. College scouts and athletic directors start looking at potential program candidates at a much younger age now. It's very competitive."

"Gordon, Gracie doesn't need a scholarship to get into college. She doesn't need scouts pursuing her at this young age. You are in a position to easily pay her tuition at any school of her choosing."

"I know that, but the athletic programs are set up in such a way that only the top athletes get in."

"What about her academic skills? Don't they count anymore?"

"Of course they do. Gracie's marks are up near the top but

she wants to advance to a career in sports. At this point, she's not sure which particular one so she has to be an excellent all-round athlete to be eligible for a school with a top notch program."

Sarah shook her head. "Young girls have enough pressure as it is without having to starve themselves and be in training seven days a week all year round. When does she get to just have some fun?"

"She did have fun these last few days, Mom. You heard her say this was the best vacation ever. You have no idea how great it was for her to spend those hours this morning on the boat. It didn't matter to her that she didn't catch a fish, it was just getting out on the water and enjoying the fresh air and sea spray."

"I suppose." Sarah spotted Gracie trotting back up the beach in her track pants and hoodie. "I just wish she could have fun for a little while every day. From what she tells me, her time is pretty regimented between school, athletics and homework."

"Sandra tells me that's the way Gracie wants it. Believe me I've questioned it but apparently that's what being a teenager is all about now."

"I get the feeling Sandra keeps pretty close tabs on Gracie. I don't think my granddaughter is allowed to make too many decisions of her own."

"Mom, cool it. There's quite a difference between today's kids and the way it was when I was growing up. Don't forget, she lives in the United States which has a different school curriculum than Canada does. Down here, if you don't have a good education from a good school, doors are harder to open. Sandra knows what it's all about and is doing her best to secure a good foundation for Gracie's future."

The bell rang announcing Gracie was waiting to be admitted downstairs which signalled the end of their conversation.

"I'm sorry if I sound like an interfering grandmother but I was hoping to see Gracie laugh more, enjoy my cooking more, be more loving. She's becoming aloof and serious. I'm glad she's going home with some happy memories of her visit here. I love you, Gordie, and I thank you for giving me some of your precious time with Gracie. I guess I'm just getting old and not as up to date with the times as I should be."

Gracie rapped on the door and Gordon let her in.

After a shower and change of clothes, Gracie rolled her suitcase to the entry way. Jake had said goodbye to the visitors earlier on the pier before hurrying to get to a tee time in another part of town.

Gracie turned and hugged her grandmother. "Thanks, Grandma. I had such a fun time. I can hardly wait until my friends see my haircut. They'll all probably want to get theirs cut short too."

Sarah held the girl close and snuck a kiss onto her cheek. "You are so special, Gracie. I love you and hope it won't be too long before we can get together for another a girls' spa day. This was the best time I've had in a long while too."

Gracie started toward the door then returned and planted a kiss on Sarah's cheek. "I love you too, Grandma."

Gordon hugged and kissed his mother then all too quickly the door closed behind them.

Strange I never noticed before how the hallway echoes when that door closes.

Chapter Ten

"Her little body was so thin when I held her."

Margaret had called from Ottawa to see how the visit was going. "Anorexia is such a problem among young girls. Psychiatrists are making a fortune. What does Gordon say about it?"

"He seems to think it's a normal part of her growing up. Apparently, she has to start training at her young age if she hopes to have an athletic career of any kind."

"Don't they need a certain amount of meat on their bones and strong muscle to be a good athlete?"

"I'm told they have to develop good eating habits early. Heaven forbid they enjoy an ice cream cone or the odd cup cake."

"Even on vacation?"

"I asked Gracie the same question and her reply was 'My mother says if you give in to the small temptations you will never be able to refuse the big ones.' So no, not even on vacation."

"Sarah, there is so much I don't understand or agree with in raising children these days. However, they seem to be surviving, even thriving, so who are we to tell them otherwise?"

"I suppose you're right, Margaret. On another note, when are you and Clarke leaving for Hawaii?"

"In a couple of days. That's why I called, to let you know that we have everything booked for the last week in February and first week in March. I'm so excited."

"Margaret, that's wonderful. I hope Clarke finds he has the stamina for it. What part of Hawaii are you going to?"

"We'll be spending the two weeks in Honolulu and tour around Oahu. We have an option for another week on Maui, maybe do some whale watching. It will depend on how Clarke is."

"It sounds divine. I hope you get to see it all."

"Have you been doing much golfing?"

"Some. The first week or so I mostly relaxed and caught up on my reading. Jake and I hit the course a few times before Gordon and Gracie arrived. I'm going to try to catch some baseball action at the training camps. One of my friends wants me to join her writing group but I don't think I can learn enough in a few short weeks to write the great Canadian novel so I may pass."

"How is Jake?"

"He's Jake — always happy and active. He arranged Gracie's first ride in a boat. We went fishing for a few hours their last morning here. That trumped anything her grandmother could offer."

"I like him, Sarah. He seems like a good friend. I'm glad you get some male companionship there at least."

"He's a friend not a boyfriend, Margaret."

"I know. I know. I'm just saying is all. You are so touchy."

"I've been married three times. I'm not about to try for four."

"Who said anything about getting married?"

"Margaret McFarland Ingram! Change the subject or I'm hanging up."

"I have to run anyway. I'll call you in a few days." The connection was closed to the sound of Margaret's laughter.

♥ ♥ ♥

"So how was Sarah when you spoke to her? Did she enjoy her granddaughter's visit?" Helen dealt the cards and sorted her own hand.

"The visit was great. She had some concern about Gracie's lack of appetite but we chalked it up to a phase the girl is going through. Apparently, she has designs on an athletic career when she's finished university and is already in training for it."

Olivia made her bid then commented, "If I remember correctly, Sarah's daughter-in-law has most of the control in that family and the little girl is pretty well under her thumb. I think Gracie will do whatever her mother decides she should do with her life. Gordon was always so busy doing what it takes to provide the lifestyle his wife enjoys so much he didn't have a lot of say in anything."

"I don't think the situation has changed much. He mostly has to visit his daughter in New York so Sarah only gets to see her granddaughter on very rare occasions. Poor Sarah, between this situation and the one with her estranged daughter, she's lucky to see any of her grandchildren more than a few times in any given year." Margaret, who had no children of her own had always felt akin to Sarah in the absence of the hugs and laughter that grandchildren bring. "I'm happy she has a good friend like Jake down there to fill her days."

"Yes, he seems to be a great guy." Helen, who was the dummy, unwrapped a chocolate kiss while the others played their hands.

Stella, who wasn't a regular asked, "Who's Jake?"

"Jake is a neighbour in the building where Sarah's condo is in Clearwater. He has become a good friend and companion to her while she's down there." Margaret tried to present Sarah's friend in as platonic a manner as she could.

"A boyfriend?"

"I wish, but no. Just a friend. They do just about everything together down there but sleep."

Helen, always the romanticist, interjected. "… And we know this for sure?"

"That they're good friends? Yes." Margaret was trying to make light of it.

"I meant do we know for sure they're not sleeping together?"

"What difference would it make anyway? Sarah is not interested in getting married again. She's had three husbands and she says that's more than enough for any woman."

"Many couples our ages share accommodations but aren't married." Stella stated matter-of-factly.

Margaret looked around at her friends. "I really can't say for certain but judging from what Sarah says, she is not interested in anything other than friendship with Jake. Whether 'friendship' involves sleepovers or not really is none of our business."

"Hmm. What a waste of a good man if they're not." Stella took the last trick which made their contract and smiled at her friends. "There are some of us who would give our eye teeth to have a good man like Jake sharing our home and/or bed. It's not fair that some get more than their share."

"Stella, are you jealous of Sarah?"

"Yes. I guess I am. I've been on my own most of my life and often wish there was a good man by my side with whom I can share my old age."

Olivia, who had remained silent throughout this exchange finally joined in. "I, too, have been on my own journey most of my life. However, I came to enjoy it. I can come and go when the mood strikes. I can opt for company or be alone with my thoughts whenever I choose. A good companion is a good companion whether it's male or female. What does it matter if it's a girlfriend, a boyfriend or just a friend? In younger years, I often wished for the constant feel of a lover in my bed but in time realized that wasn't going to happen. The few times I had an opportunity, it just didn't seem worth giving up my privacy for. If Sarah is happy with her relationship with Jake just the way it is, then that's her choice. They're together when they want to be, sleeping or not, and they're separate when they want. As soon as you 'move in together' that changes the whole dynamic of the relationship and obligates each person to a certain behaviour or pattern. Not for me."

She realized the others around the table were staring at her. She had always been a very private person and this was the most open and lengthy exchange of her personal lifestyle they had ever heard from her. "Now, are we playing cards or aren't we?"

Stella shuffled the cards as Helen talked about the robin she had spotted on her walk along the canal the day before. "First of the season."

Chapter Eleven

The month of March was almost gone. Sarah had developed her usual medium tan. Jake had what he called "farmers' arms" with a tan that started below his short sleeves. Neither one was the sitting-around-the-pool sort, each preferring shade rather than bright sun. What they got on the golf course was enough. None of Sarah's friends from Ottawa had come down for a visit this year, nor had either of her grandsons who lived in Toronto.

They had just enjoyed sharing a steak dinner at Jake's place. He didn't cook very much but sometimes had dinner brought in for the two of them.

"Ya know, Sarah, I've been thinking …"

"Oh oh. No good can come from that."

He smiled when she patted his shoulder.

"What have you been thinking, Jake?"

"It's a long drive back. Why don't you travel with me and keep me company in the car then fly home from Chicago?"

"What? I thought you always enjoyed the solitude of the drive."

"I always have but somehow this time the drive home seems more daunting. Maybe I should start thinking of flying down here instead of driving."

"Then you won't have the luxury of a car while you're here."

"I can always rent or lease one for the couple months I'm here."

"That's true."

"Whaddaya say? Will you ride with me?"

"Can I think about it? I'm not great on long-haul drives. That's why I've been flying back and forth all these years."

He slid an arm around her shoulders and pulled her until her head rested on his shoulder. "Yes, of course you can think about it. I'd enjoy your company. We can take our time. Have you ever been through the Smoky Mountains in Tennessee?"

"Nope."

"How about the farms in Kentucky? There are some beautiful horse farms there."

"I've always flown over the United States. I've been to very few places."

"Well, then let me show them to you."

"Is Nashville along the route?"

"It could be. It very definitely could be." He kissed her temple and stood up. "Okay, this old guy is throwing you out now. I have an early tee time tomorrow and I have to beat the asshole who set it up."

"What? Why is he an asshole?"

"For arranging a seven o'clock tee time when we're both retired and could just as easily have started at eleven o'clock. He needs his ass whumped for that."

"I feel sorry for him and don't forget to replace the divots because I have a feeling the fairways are going to be victimized by you taking out your mad, somehow, for the early start."

He walked her to the door where she slid her arms around his waist. "I'll think about joining you for the long ride home."

"I hope so, darlin'. I'll beat this guy real quick and come by later to take you out for a late breakfast."

It was barely eight o'clock when a knock on Sarah's door

woke her up. She peeked through the peep hole to see Jake leaning against the door.

"What happened to your golf game?"

"The asshole phoned first thing this morning telling me that his wife needed him to drive her to a flea market somewhere. I waited until I felt it was a decent hour to come calling. I brought flowers and everything for waking you up." He handed her a bouquet that she knew had come from the counter in the lobby of their building.

"Does Dorothy know you've stolen her flowers?"

"I didn't steal them. I just borrowed them. We'll put them back on our way out."

Sarah snorted she was laughing so hard. "Jake, you sure know how to start a girl's day with a laugh."

"I figured if I come knocking this early, I better come bearing gifts."

"You are the gift. You don't need to give me anything else."

"You always make me feel special. I'll put some coffee on while you get dressed. I'm not going to let a cancelled golf game with an asshole ruin our day." He kissed her forehead and the tip of her nose.

She heard him shuffling pots and cutlery in the kitchen and when she stepped out of the shower, the smell of frying bacon drew her into the kitchen. He had decided to cook breakfast for them. They ate on the balcony and watched as a family played in the shallow water with a toddler whose giggle carried up to their floor every time a waved lapped at his round little belly.

"Let's not go anywhere today. Why don't we just sit here and do a puzzle or something? I'm too lazy to do anything but relax and enjoy the view from your balcony." Jake put his feet up and leaned back on the chaise.

"Hmm. I'll go along with that. In fact, today might be a good day to browse through travel brochures."

"Travel brochures? What kind of travel brochures?" He sat upright.

"Do you know how many places on how many islands there are to visit in Hawaii?"

A surprised grin spread across Jake's normally calm features.

Sarah fanned out several colourful folders that she had picked up a few days previous. "Of course, the choices vary by the time of year we choose to be there."

"I choose tomorrow."

Chapter Twelve

The next week was spent cleaning and getting her condo ready for the tenants that would be renting through the property managers while she was in Canada. Professional cleaners would come before vacationers would arrive, but Sarah always gave the place a light going-over after she had stowed some of her personal belongings in the storage locker in the basement.

She had decided to take Jake up on his suggestion that they drive together to Chicago. They both had spent less time than normal in Florida this year and the idea of spending a few more days together might extend what they thought of as their winter vacation. She cancelled her flight and received a credit with the airline. It could possibly be applied toward their proposed trip to Hawaii. The sun was shining and the weatherman promised several more days of pleasant weather as they were about to make their way up the central-eastern portion of the United States.

"You travel light. I thought a woman like you would have half a dozen suitcases." He looked at her two pieces of luggage in the hallway.

"I leave a lot of my stuff here in storage so that I don't have to tote it back and forth." She looked him in the eye. "What do you mean by 'a woman like me'?"

"You're always so well-dressed and up-to-date with the latest fashions."

"The latest fashions down here don't change much. Shorts, capris and T-shirts with the occasional sundress for dinner out. Add a couple pairs of sandals and tennis shoes and that's all I need."

"You make it sound simple but you always look so well done up."

She smiled at his compliment and locked the door to her condo. "Let's get this show on the road. How far are we going today?"

"As far as we feel like driving."

"No hotel reservations made anywhere?"

"Nope. Reservations are for people on a timetable. We're retired. If we feel like calling it a day, we'll stop. If we feel like going another hundred miles, we'll keep going. We've got blue skies, Sirius to give us a choice of music and lots of country to enjoy."

"Sounds like heaven."

They cleared the outskirts of the city by mid-morning and headed in the general direction of The Smoky Mountains in Tennessee. Jake was right. The skies couldn't be bluer and he found several channels on Sirius to suit both their tastes in music. He was an easy person to travel with. They rode many miles in silence, enjoying the countryside and the sheer pleasure of each other's company. He set the cruise control about five miles above the posted speed limit, stopping several times to point out landmarks and local tourist sights he thought she'd enjoy. They stopped for lunch in Lake City then crossed into Georgia. At six o'clock they took a room at an inn just off the highway in Macon.

Jake booked them into adjoining rooms, each with a king-size bed. They opened onto a courtyard with a small outdoor pool. After tossing around several options, they decided to have a leisurely evening on the patio with drinks and room service.

"Did you know there's an Allman Brothers Band Museum in Macon?" Jake was sitting on the sofa removing his shoes.

"Can't say that I ever knew that." Sarah was drying her hair after a refreshing shower. She smiled at Jake. "Who are the Allman Brothers?"

"Well, darlin', they were pretty big in the late '60s and early '70s. Then one of them got killed. I think right here in Macon. Anyway, they seemed to break up and start up again routinely. I think they still appear at different places around the country. I'm surprised you don't even recognize the name of the band but they had some pretty big hits back when. I think they lived here for a while. Just a bit of local trivia for ya."

He went into the other bedroom and Sarah heard the shower going. She mixed a drink for herself and took it out to the table on the patio outside the sliding door. She thought about their day. She hadn't been sure she'd enjoy travelling by car but Jake was a good driver and a great travel companion. Knowing they still had a long way to go, she was relieved and happy to have enjoyed this first day so much. It had been relaxing, stopping whenever they pleased and not having any destination they absolutely had to reach by any given time. He had mentioned they would reach the Smoky Mountains tomorrow and maybe spend some time in the National Park. She would have to remember to wear good walking shoes.

"Would you like to see anything around Macon before we leave tomorrow? There are several museums here including an ancient Indian site."

"Why don't we see what we feel up to in the morning? I think I'd rather move on and spend time in the mountains but if there's something you want to see here, we can do that."

They enjoyed their dinner then took a walk to a convenience store to buy snacks to eat in the car the next day. Jake kissed her goodnight and settled into bed while she watched the late news on television and part of Stephen Colbert before falling asleep.

It was the smell of coffee that woke her up. Jake had brewed the little pot that was in his room.

"I can't believe that it's morning already. I zonked out with the television still on last night." She joined him on the sofa with a glass of orange juice.

"I know. I heard you snoring right through the wall."

"I don't snore."

"Yes. You do."

"I do not snore."

"Well, then you had somebody in here with you because there was definitely snoring coming from this room." He bent and kissed her as he handed her a mug of steaming coffee.

"I hope it didn't keep you awake."

"No. Don't worry, I'm well-rested and ready to drive. I like your idea of moving on and spending our time enjoying the mountain views. It's been a while since I slipped over to the east part of Tennessee. I usually drive down through Nashville."

He shaved then brought his suitcase to the door. "Do you want to grab something from the complimentary breakfast here? We can pick up something more substantial down the road later."

"I usually just have a muffin with fruit or something. What about you?"

"That suits me fine."

"I'll put my face on while you grab a couple muffins from the breakfast room then."

She heard the door open as she zipped her suitcase shut. He had two white bags with something inside that smelled delicious. He set them on the table and watched her check herself in the mirror on the door. "You look beautiful, as always."

He moved closer and slid his arms around her waist. She stepped into his embrace and kissed him softly. He didn't release his hold. "I'm going to have a hard time saying goodbye when you get on that plane in Chicago."

"Then you'll just have to make a trip to Ottawa over the summer."

He stared into her eyes. "I guess I could do that." He squeezed her then reached for her suitcase. "We better get out of here before the maid comes in and catches us making whoopee."

"Making whoopee?" Sarah laughed. "Jake, for such a cool guy, you sure come out with some old-fashioned sayings."

"Ah, darlin', I'm just an old-fashioned guy at heart."

He found a drive-through to pick up two coffees to wash down their bacon-and-cheese-flavoured biscuits on their way out of town. They skirted Atlanta then left the highway they had been travelling on for another that headed north toward North Carolina and the Smokies. It would be a much shorter drive today but more stopping for sightseeing.

They ended up staying the night in Bryson City, Tennessee. The views had been spectacular. Sarah had suffered from vertigo more than once. The lookout sights were dizzying at some points and Sarah did not do heights well. However, the colours of the mountains and the trees and valleys were more than she had expected. Late that afternoon when they finally checked in to a motel room on the highway, they were both exhausted from all the hiking and walking required.

"After today, I can finally admit that I am definitely not as young as I used to be." Sarah threw herself onto one of the beds.

"Glad to hear you say that, Sarah, because I'm too tired to pretend I'm still a robust mountain man." He sat on the edge of the other bed and loosened the laces in his hiking boots.

She reached for him. "Come and lay beside me. I feel a nap coming on."

"Really darlin'?"

"I just want to relax for a while. All that grandeur we experienced today has me somewhat overwhelmed. It felt like I was in a different world. The mountains, the valleys, the colours and wildlife, the views so far down they make you feel like you're above it all. Floating. It was truly a heavenly experience. I need to be held and anchored. Nothing more than that, Jake."

He lay down beside her and placed her head on his shoulder. "Then close your eyes, darlin', and I'll sing you a soothing lullaby."

Chapter Thirteen

"So what's this about Sarah flying out of Chicago? What's she doing in Chicago?" Stella was addressing the women sitting around her dining room table playing their bi-weekly game of bridge.

Margaret, who had just laid her dummy hand down, explained. "Jake talked her into riding up to Chicago with him. Sarah has never gone by car through the States so she decided to give it a try."

"How long would that take? A couple of days?" Stella was near making contract but was interested in finding out more.

"I would guess three at least. I think they're taking their time, though, and doing some sightseeing along the way."

"She sent a brief text last night to say she was exhausted. Apparently, they did some walking in the Smoky Mountains yesterday. I wouldn't be surprised if they don't stay in Nashville for an extra day or two." Olivia stole a trick from Stella.

"Way to go, Olivia." Helen smiled at her partner as she gathered the cards in. "Nashville is a great place to spend some time. I hope she gets to hear people she likes at the Grand Ole Opry."

"See, now that's what I mean. She is so lucky to have someone she can just go where she wants with. She has the security of a man with her, someone to talk with and she gets to sit back and enjoy the scenery. I'm trying not to be jealous but I can't help it."

"Stella, if it's the travel you want and the company of others, there are any number of interesting bus tours that will take you all over North America." Helen shuffled the cards.

"I don't want to go with a bunch of strangers. I want to travel with someone I know. Someone I have something in common with and with whom I'm comfortable sharing a seat for sixteen hours a day. Besides they're mostly old retired people."

The friends looked each other up and down and burst into laughter.

"One of the women who lives on the eleventh floor went on a tour a few years ago and came back with the nicest man. He joined the tour in Toronto and they hit it off immediately. I think they went through the Rocky Mountains right down to San Diego and came back through Las Vegas. They travel back and forth on the train to see each other often and have gone on another bus tour together since then. You know Elizabeth Turcotte I think, Margaret?"

"Yes. You're right. I do remember that. They're still seeing each other?"

"As often as they can. Neither will move closer because her family is here and his in southern Ontario."

"I'm sorry. I can't help envying Sarah her Jake. You girls make him sound like such a nice guy. I wish I could find my own Jake."

"Take a bus ride. Maybe you will. Or next time Sarah offers her condo down there, take her up on it and go down for a few weeks or a month."

"Maybe I will. Maybe I just will. Now, let's get this card game done so I can share my new dessert with you over coffee."

♥ ♥ ♥

"Poor Stella. She sure hasn't had an easy life." Helen always felt guilty about a misunderstanding a few years earlier. It had been an embarrassing situation for them all. The only good that came out of it was that Stella became closer with the group when it could have easily gone the other way.

"Some of us are okay on our own, but unfortunately, she's not one. I wish there was some way we could help her. Friendship isn't enough. She needs a life companion." Olivia had been alone for as long as they had all been neighbours and was quite content.

Helen nodded in agreement. "Maybe we can talk her into going to Florida or even taking a bus tour and engaging in activities that include men. She has so much to offer. Her baking alone is enough to keep any man happy."

"Let's work on it." The elevator doors closed behind Olivia.

Chapter Fourteen

Sarah and Jake spent two days and nights in Nashville. Before noon on the third day, they hit the I-65 and headed toward Indianapolis. Once there, they'd decide whether to spend another night on the road or to keep going the extra three hours to Chicago. However, fate reared its ugly head in the form of a phone call from Gordon.

"Hi, Gordon. Are you wondering where I am?"

"Well, yes, in a way."

"We're in Kentucky, nearing Louisville. You wouldn't believe the scenery and the beautiful horse farms we are driving by."

"Mom, I hate to interrupt your vacation but something has happened."

"Happened? What is it dear?"

"There's been an accident and Sandra is on life support in the hospital. I'm in the Montreal airport now waiting to board a flight. Gracie is with Sandra's mother at the hospital. I ... I ... Are you able to get to New York to help with Gracie?" His voice broke. "It doesn't sound good, Mom."

"Oh, no. Of course, I'll come. Let me see where I can get a plane from and I'll get back to you."

"Thank you. They're calling my flight now so I'll check in with you when I get into New York."

"Give everyone my love and tell Gracie I'll be there as quick as I can." She knew that Gordon had never stopped loving his wife. "And sweetheart, I love you. Hang in there."

When they broke the connection, Sarah realized that Jake had pulled in to the parking lot of a truck stop.

"What's up, darling?"

"It's Gordon's ex-wife. I didn't get details as he was boarding a flight but apparently she was badly injured in an accident of some kind. I didn't think to ask but I'm assuming it was a car accident. He needs me in New York to help with Gracie."

She looked around at the vehicles and trucks in the large parking lot. "Where are we? Is there somewhere close by that I can find a plane to New York?"

"Probably the closest airport is the one in Louisville. It's about forty-five minutes away. Do you want to call ahead and see when you can get a flight?"

She was looking at her contacts on her cell phone. "I'll call my travel agent in Ottawa and have her make all the arrangements for me."

"Good thinking. Do you want to get something to drink and take a washroom break while we're here? Then I'll just drive straight to the airport when we get there."

"That's probably a good idea."

While she placed the call to Donna, her travel agent, Jake found a parking spot closer to the entrance to the busy restaurant. By the time they had eaten, she had confirmation of a seat on a flight leaving at four o'clock that afternoon. Jake had offered to fly with her, but she declined, not knowing what was waiting for her in New York.

Hwy 65 conveniently took them right to the airport. They arrived in good time and Jake insisted on having his car parked and going in with her. "I can't just leave you in a strange airport, especially you being Canadian and all. I'll feel better once you're through security and I know you'll be okay."

She couldn't help but smile wondering whether he thought the airport attendants might not understand her Canadian accent. But she did appreciate his concern and support.

"So will you just take a taxi to the hospital or what?"

"I expect to hear from Jake before I have to board and he'll let me know. I would imagine so. He said Sandra was on life support, so I don't even know what to expect. Maybe Gracie will want to stay at the hospital. I can only guess the state Sandra's mother must be in if her daughter is fighting for her life."

He walked with her to the entrance to security. "Thank you, Jake, for everything. I'm so sorry we didn't get to finish the trip." She stepped into his arms and kissed his cheek.

"You just take care of yourself, Sarah. I think I'll keep going to Chicago so call me later tonight and let me know how things are, okay?" He gave her a warm hug and kissed her soundly on her mouth. "I love you, darlin'. You take of yourself and that little girl."

Sarah was sitting in the secured area awaiting the call to board when her phone beeped and Gordon's name appeared on the screen. "Mom, I just cleared customs and I'm getting into a cab. Sandra is at Bellevue Hospital. I don't know my way around there yet so have an airport cab take you to the main entrance of the hospital and call me from there. I guess you have luggage too. God, this is a mess. Poor Gracie."

"What kind of accident was it?"

"She was in taxi that was broadsided by a big truck of some kind. She's just barely hanging on. The doctors are waiting to talk to me, so I don't know what's happening exactly."

"Okay, son. They're boarding my plane now so I'll call you when I arrive at the hospital. Stay strong."

"Call me from the airport in New York in case things change." His voice broke again. "Mom, thanks so much for dropping everything and coming in such a hurry."

"I'll see you soon. Feel my hug."

She had given Margaret's phone number to Jake so he could call and tell her friends what was happening. He was to explain that she'd call them when she knew anything but she wanted to keep her line free and her battery charged until she was settled in somewhere.

At her first opportunity she called Gordon from the airport in New York. "She's gone, Mom. Sandra didn't make it."

"Oh my. Gordon, I am so sorry. Did you get to see her?"

"Yes. She was on life support but they removed it soon after I arrived. The poor woman was so badly injured she just didn't stand a chance."

"How is Gracie?"

"She's in a state of shock. We're just on our way home. Sandra's mother and dad have gone home to be by themselves for a bit."

"Shall I take a cab to Sandra's or should I go to a hotel?"

"Come to Sandra's and we'll sit and decide what we're going to do. I think you have the address?"

"Yes. I'll see you soon."

It was nearing midnight by the time they had gone through the emotional explanations of what had happened. Gracie was almost inconsolable. She seemed even thinner than she'd looked just weeks before.

There was enough room in the apartment for all of them. Sarah would take the guest room and Gordon would sleep in Sandra's room. Gracie had her own room. They lived in a beautiful large building, just blocks from Central Park. The snow was mostly gone, only a trace left here and there. They had suffered the same cold winter that Eastern Ontario had gone through. Elizabeth and George were coming over in the morning to discuss funeral arrangements. It was already known that Sandra wanted to be cremated. She had often said that she didn't want people staring at her in a coffin. Her wishes would be respected.

Sarah had called Jake with the news once they were all settled and she'd been able to shower and put clean clothes on. Now she was alone in her room and called Margaret about the change of course the day had taken.

She had been asleep only a couple of hours when she heard a soft voice whisper in her ear. "Grandma, can I sleep with you?"

Chapter Fifteen

Sarah was first one up and had the coffee maker going when she heard Gordon come into the kitchen. "Were you able to sleep, son?"

He placed an arm around her shoulders and a kiss on her temple. "Surprisingly, yes." He looked toward the hallway. "I wonder if Gracie did."

"She slept with me. I guess she felt terribly alone in her room and came to me for comfort in the middle of the night."

"That's a relief, Mom. I was afraid she might retreat into a shell. She didn't say much at the hospital, just sat by herself crying and not letting anyone touch her."

"She and Sandra were very close. It's going to be hard for her going forward."

"I know. There'll be lots of changes for her, I'm afraid. I was thinking last night that she'll have to move to Canada and that will be a big change. Then of course the cultural differences between New York and Montreal." He sat at the table where Sarah poured a cup of coffee for him. "I don't want to hit her with everything all at once, so we'll have to discuss these changes one at a time."

Gracie got up shortly before her grandparents arrived. She appeared to have slept soundly once she fell asleep. Sarah had felt her thin body through her pyjama bottoms and over-sized T-shirt when the child had snuggled against her in a hug.

"Will you have some toast, sweetie?"

"No, thank you. I'll make a smoothie for myself." She reached for a banana.

Sarah hugged the young girl. "Bananas are full of potassium. I should be eating more of them myself." She could see Gordon's shoulders relax when she didn't chide Gracie for not eating something more hardy.

When Elizabeth and George Chalmers arrived, Sarah scrambled some eggs and microwaved some turkey sausages. They sat at the dining room table to discuss the funeral arrangements. Sarah was wise enough to leave Gordon and his in-laws to make all the decisions. Sandra had been spouse and daughter to all of them and had not been close to Sarah at all. Gracie made a suggestion here and there about flowers and food for the reception. She knew her mother's taste and was quite certain what the woman would have wanted. When her grandparents didn't agree with a number of things, Gracie stuck to her guns and insisted. She got the backing of her father and so it went on until lunch time. The funeral director from the chosen chapel arrived after lunch to help with the choice of urn for the ashes and took care of all the arrangements for the service and burial.

Watching from a spectator's point of view, Sarah was impressed with Gracie's decision-making and the way she took command of many aspects. No shrinking violet this girl. She was not going to be coerced into anything that her father or grandparents wanted that she knew her mother wouldn't have liked. The phone calls and flowers from friends started arriving by late afternoon. Gracie and Elizabeth sat together and worked on the obituary for the papers. Gordon insisted it be given to him for final approval.

The funeral was set for four days later. Sarah handled the meals and went to the deli and market that Gracie suggested. Two days had passed in no time flat. The day before the funeral,

Margaret called to let her know that she and Olivia were flying down that evening to attend the service.

"Margaret, that's really nice of you and Olivia to do this. Gordon will be happy to know you are offering your condolences in person."

"Yes, well, it's the least we can do. Besides, we've been dying to see *Cats* so we've already got our tickets for that. Any chance you might join us?"

Sarah laughed. "I wish I could, but it wouldn't look very nice for me to be in mourning by day and carousing around Broadway at night."

"I suppose."

"Please make time to come to the apartment after the service and have some tea with us. I miss you girls and would like some time with you. Say, would you be able to bring me a few changes of clothes? All I have are casual things from Florida. I didn't pack anything to wear around New York."

"Sure, we can do that. Text me a list of what you want and we'll bring an extra suitcase. Do you need shoes or a winter coat?"

"I'll try to keep it down to one suitcase, but I'll send you a list. My big Pullman is in the closet in the guest room."

"Do you know how long you'll be staying there?"

"We haven't really talked about it. We wanted to get through the funeral before Gordon and Gracie decide what to do about her future. There's Sandra's will and the apartment and all that to take care of also. I really don't know what's going to happen. Poor kid. She's been holding up really well."

"How have the in-laws been?"

"Excellent. They respect that Gordon is Gracie's dad and that he was married to Sandra. He never stopped loving her, you know. I'll never figure out what attracted him to her besides her good looks, but he only had eyes for her. Well, you know how devastated he was when she decided to call it quits. I think the Chalmers respect him for that. He always did get along well with George. I'd better run, I understand that some of Sandra's friends are stopping by this afternoon so I want to have some baking ready."

"You are amazing. I'd be losing steam after all the travelling with Jake and then the catastrophe of Sandra's death and caring for everyone there but you can only think about what to bake next. I'll let you go and we'll call when we're in town with your clothes."

Sarah was happy that her friends were coming. It gave her spirits a lift. She knew she owed Jake a phone call also but would call him after she had a few things baked.

Chapter Sixteen

Margaret and Olivia had sent her clothes over in a taxi. They had packed well and had even fit a heavy spring coat in the bag. Sarah felt more comfortable in her business attire rather than the capris and cotton pants she'd been wearing around the apartment.

On the morning of the funeral, Gracie was visibly distraught. She had been putting on a good front but Sarah had seen she was stressed by all the company and forced smiles. It was good that today would bring closure and the girl could move on. Several of her school friends had been spending time with her and she seemed to relax a little when they were around. Her gymnastics coach had called to make sure she was at least getting some of her floor exercises and her running done. If it had been up to Sarah, she would have intercepted those calls and let the girl enjoy some time without the stress of commitments.

They arrived at the chapel an hour ahead of the service to receive friends wanting to express condolences. Sarah sat in the row behind the family and Gracie had turned to talk to her when the young girl's face lit up in a smile. "Hi, Mr. Tatarek." She stood and went into the aisle. Sarah turned, and sure enough, there was Jake sitting a couple rows behind. Gracie insisted he move up to sit with Sarah.

"What are you doing here?"

"Ah, I was sitting at home thinking about you being here

under all this stress and I just wanted to see for myself that you're okay. Maybe there's something I can do for you."

"Jake, that's so sweet."

Gordon turned and saw Jake and started to stand but Jake raised his hand. "Stay there, young fella."

Jake walked to the front row and shook Gordon's hand, offering his condolences. Gordon then introduced him to Sandra's parents and her brother, all of whom were surprised when Gracie took his hand and led him to the pedestal table to show him the picture of her mother placed by the urn containing her ashes.

"Your momma was a beautiful lady."

"Yes, she was. I hope I'll be as beautiful as her."

"Ah, child. You're already a beauty even though you look more like your daddy." He smiled at her. "Been thinking about doing any fishing this spring?"

"I'd love to."

"We'll see what we can do." He walked her back to her seat and eased into the one beside Sarah. At that moment, Sarah heard a couple of female voices. "Jake, what are you doing here?" Margaret and Olivia had arrived. The friends all embraced one another and then offered condolences to the family in front of them.

The service wasn't long. Three people had been asked to give remembrances and all appeared to have a high regard for the woman who had died so tragically. Lunch was served in a reception room down the hall from the chapel. Several people were invited to the apartment for further conversation with the family. Among the invited guests were Sarah's friends. Jake had a flight out later that evening, but the two women were staying in town to attend the Broadway play.

Sarah had been given a reprieve from cooking and baking, as a caterer had been hired to prepare food and serve the invited guests. It was mid-afternoon by the time the apartment was mostly empty. A few hangers-on were still conversing softly with the Chalmers and Jake was sitting with Sarah. "How was your flight, darlin'?"

"I honestly don't remember. I got on the plane and I got off the plane. Nothing registered in between. All I could think of was what lay ahead for me here. All kinds of scenarios were playing themselves out in my mind."

"And you arrived to the worst one possible."

"I don't see it that way. She was so badly injured that had she survived, she would never have been a whole person — the person she was before. I think God, in his goodness, took her without her suffering a long and painful life and sparing the family the torment of watching her suffer."

"I guess that is a good way of looking at it."

"I can't imagine that Sandra would have liked to live like that. She was such a vibrant, busy person, it would have been a very slow death for her."

"How's the little one holding up?"

"She's been surprisingly strong. I keep waiting for her to break. Maybe now that the funeral is over she will. Then again maybe she won't. She's a trooper."

Jake took her hand. "She's got her grandmama's blood in her."

Sarah looked at his hand holding hers. "Thank you for coming, Jake. It really means a lot to me."

He lifted her hand to his lips. "I wanted to be here. I needed to be here."

"So when are you going to take me fishing again?" Gracie sat on the ottoman in front of them.

"Well, little lady, that's up to you and your daddy. You don't have to go all the way to Florida for fishing. I can take you fishing on Lake Michigan."

"Or you can take her fishing in the Adirondacks or the St. Lawrence River." Gordon joined his daughter on the ottoman.

"Wow. So many choices. Does that mean I can take another week off from school, Dad?"

"No, young lady, it does not. But you will have a whole summer to go fishing. Surely we can find a few days suitable to all."

"Can Grandma come, Jake?"

"Only if she promises to cook our catch."

Her grandparents called her over then to say goodbye to them and the final stragglers. After the door closed, the apartment seemed so quiet. Only the sound of the caterers cleaning up could be heard. Gracie looked around at the three sitting in a close circle. And burst into tears.

Chapter Seventeen

Two weeks later, Sarah and Stella were enjoying lunch in Olivia's condo. A snowstorm was once again hitting the nation's capital region. This one was laced with freezing rain. Advisories against driving in the current weather conditions were being broadcast every thirty minutes on the news.

"Days like this make me wish I had stayed in Florida until the end of April." Olivia picked up their lunch plates after setting a platter of butter tarts in the centre of the table.

"Why don't you stay down there for the complete winter, Olivia?" Stella was always curious about people who had the means to travel and didn't.

"I really don't know. I can't say it's because I enjoy our winters here. I guess I'm just a home body and like my own familiar space."

"But if you stayed there for six months, you might be as familiar with your space there as here."

"I suppose. I can't imagine being away for that length of time. What about you Sarah? Have you ever thought about wintering down south?"

"No. I do enjoy the couple of months I'm there but I'm always so happy to come home again."

"Even if Jake stayed there all winter too?"

"Even if."

"Does Jake ever make his way up to Ottawa?"

"No. Although he's talking about possibly making a trip up this spring. He and Gordon have talked about the four of us taking a fishing trip together."

"Four of you?" Stella wore a surprised expression.

"Yes. Gordon, Gracie, Jake and me."

"Oh, of course. I forgot he knows your son and granddaughter."

"Sounds like a family to me." Olivia winked at Sarah.

"Jake took quite a liking to Gracie. He doesn't get to see his grandchildren too often. She seemed to fill a void when they met and he felt so bad when her mother died."

"I think he has taken quite a liking to Gracie's grandmother also. I guess that explains his need to travel to New York for Sandra's funeral. He was giving his sympathy to both you and Gracie. I guess he's pretty familiar with Gordon too."

"Yes. They've met several times. Gordon enjoyed the morning of fishing during Gracie's visit and they agreed they'd like to do it again. Jake hasn't fished in Canada so he's really looking forward to it."

"Will he go directly to Montreal or will he come here first?"

"He'll probably fly or drive here. He's never been to Ottawa before and thought he'd like to do a few tourist things here before we go fishing." She looked at both women. "And before you ask, he'll be staying with me here. We're used to sharing living space. We stayed together on our road trip last month and we're planning a trip to Hawaii in the near future too. I would like him to meet Clarke and listen to their stories about the Hawaiian Islands."

Before Stella could get the words out, Sarah continued. "I'd like you to meet him, too, Stella. You and Helen are the only friends of mine he doesn't know. Maybe I'll have a dinner party while he's here."

"I'd like that a lot, Sarah." Even after several years, Stella always seemed to be so grateful and happy to be included in their friendship circle. "Do you have a date or timeframe in mind?"

"Nothing definite. As you know, it was decided that Gracie would finish her school year at her current school. Gordon is, for the most part, carrying on his business dealings during the week from New York with Sandra's parents helping with the girl's schedule for sporting events and time spent with her close friends. Gordon slips home here and there and on weekends to do what needs to be done in and from Montreal. That large apartment in New York will be placed on the market once school is out and Gracie moves to Montreal. School lets out earlier in the United States than it does in Canada so she could be settled into her dad's home by early June. We'll plan something for soon after she moves in."

"How does she feel about moving to Canada?" Olivia's voice was cautious.

"She hates to leave her friends and her sport teammates but I think she's good with coming to live with her dad. She's more concerned about her sports opportunities in this country than she is about leaving her friends, I think."

Stella was deep in thought. "I would guess the whole school curriculum would be different. She wouldn't know much about Canadian history or politics so she'll have some catching up to do."

"Yes, I guess so. We're hoping a week in a cottage complete with a fishing boat might help to ease the anxiety of leaving her home and school behind. Gordon offered to accommodate one of her best friends for the week if Gracie would like to invite someone her own age along."

"It sounds like everything is under control. I'm quite envious. I used to enjoy fishing with my parents when I was a youngster. I hope Gracie and her dad are able to start a new tradition." Stella seemed quite genuine in her well wishes.

Chapter Eighteen

The freezing weather continued. It was the topic of almost every conversation and left an aura of gloom over the whole city. Soon tidbits of purple could be seen here and there in the residential and suburban areas as the crocuses braved the frigid temperatures and poked their lavender and purple bonnets above ground. Gordon suggested that Sarah fly down to New York for Easter so that Gracie could celebrate the holiday in the home familiar to her before it was sold. Sandra's parents were also grateful they could share the occasion with their granddaughter in their daughter's home for the last time.

"Do you think Jake would come if we invited him?"

Gracie's affection for Jake was becoming increasingly apparent. She asked about him often and seemed genuinely interested in his well-being.

"I don't know, sweetie. I'm not sure what his plans are. Did you check this out with your other grandparents? Maybe they would prefer Easter just be celebrated with family."

"Grandma, Jake is almost family. Besides he's all alone. Don't you think he'd like to be with us for the holiday? If you give me his number, I'll ask him myself."

"How about running it by your grandma and grandpa Chalmers first?"

An audible sigh preceded the young girl's response. "Okay. But I know they'll say yes."

"You're probably right, dear, but I think they'll appreciate being asked."

A few phone calls later it was confirmed that Jake would join them in New York for Easter weekend.

"So, all of a sudden Jake seems to be an important part of your family gatherings." Olivia smiled as she dealt the cards.

"What do you mean?" Helen's curiosity was sparked.

Margaret answered Helen's question. "Sarah is going to New York to join Gordon and Gracie and the in-laws for Easter dinner and it seems Jake has been included in the family feast — at Gracie's request."

"Really?" Helen looked at Sarah. "That's a serious inclusion, isn't it?"

Sarah paused before answering. "You must remember that it's Gracie's invitation, not mine. The man entered her life at a vulnerable time and she took to his kind, gentle manner instantly. He offered a change of focus when she needed to be diverted from the direction her life was taking. She was becoming stressed over needing to be at the top of her game, needing to be physically at her best, needing to be accepted by her peers both at school and in her athletics and, unfortunately, by her mother's need for her to be perfect, by her maternal grandmother's need for her to be accepted into the school the women in their family had all attended. Of course, I added to her stress by admonishing her at every opportunity for not eating properly, by not getting enough sun. Then along came Jake who showed an interest in her wants, not her needs, and took her fishing — on a boat — something her own grandmother was not even aware she had never been on." She put her cards down without sorting them.

"Jake showed her how to bait a line. He delighted in her squeals of joy when she got a bite then showed her how to set the hook and reel it in. He listened to her when she talked. He hugged her when she kissed him on the cheek — a show of affection I rarely received from her. He didn't care if she was too thin or if her school marks were slipping or if she was too pale for someone having just spent a few days in Florida. He simply took pleasure from the moments shared with a delightful child who was experiencing a new kind of fun for the first time. He was being what a grandparent should be. A loving, caring being who just wanted her to enjoy herself, no strings attached. It didn't matter if they were fishing or if they'd been flying kites in a desert, they were doing something just for the sheer pleasure of it, not for the need to be the best at it. He was being something this grandma forgot how to be. It's no surprise she wants him there for her first Easter without her mother. It's no surprise she loves him like a grandfather.

"So ... let's play cards before you have me married again." She picked up her cards and started sorting them while her friends tried to hide their smiles.

Chapter Nineteen

Jake arrived in New York late in the afternoon on Holy Saturday. Gracie was disappointed that he had rented a car at the airport which cancelled the need to be met and chauffeured to their apartment.

"You know we would have picked you up, Jake. Dad and I were all prepared to go."

"Believe me, Gracie, the parking lot at a New York airport on a holiday weekend is one place to avoid if at all possible. It was easier this way. They brought the car to the door and I just drove away. Thank you for the offer though." He bent to accept her kiss on the cheek.

"It was nice of you to invite me to stay here in the apartment with you this weekend, son." He turned to Gordon as Gracie hung his jacket in the foyer closet.

"We have lots of room, Jake, and it's more convenient to park your car here than at a hotel — quite a bit cheaper too."

Sarah offered her cheek to her friend but he took her face in his hands and placed his lips on hers. She was surprised to feel herself blushing.

"Come and sit down." Gracie guided Jake into the large living room.

"I didn't notice this the last time I was here." He gestured toward a baby grand piano in the corner of the room by a pair of floor-to-ceiling windows.

"It was in the den before but my grandma had it moved out here so she could listen to me play."

"You play the piano, kiddo?"

"Yes. Grandma says it rounds out my portfolio." She rolled her eyes. "Who even uses that word 'portfolio'?"

"Obviously, grandmas do." He turned to Sarah. "I didn't know you were interested in piano music. Do you play?"

"No. It's her Grandmother Chalmers she's referring to."

"What kind of music do you play?" Jake turned to Gracie again.

"Classical." The young girl barely whispered it.

"How far have you gone in your music study?"

"I'm in grade six. I didn't want to study it at all so I got a late start when Grandma Chalmers kept insisting on it."

"Don't you enjoy it?"

"Not really." She turned to her dad. "I hope I don't have to continue with music lessons after we move. Please tell me we're not taking the piano with us."

"Gracie, you have come so far it would be a shame to quit now."

The girl didn't argue but she lowered her head.

"I haven't touched the keys in years. Would you mind if I gave it a try?"

The young face lifted in surprise. "You play the piano?"

"Well, I'm probably nowhere near as accomplished as you but I used to play a tune or two." He walked toward the piano. "May I?"

He looked at both Gordon and Gracie.

"Sure!" The girl's enthusiasm gave him the permission he was looking for even before Gordon nodded in consent.

He played around with a few keys and winked at Sarah as the tinkling sounds became Billy Joel's *Piano Man*. Halfway through, the beat changed to Fats Domino's *Blueberry Hill*. When he changed the tempo to Jerry Lee Lewis, Gracie shrieked and joined him on the bench. She started tapping out a chord in time to his music.

Gordon looked at his mother and smiled. She breathed a sigh of relief, afraid he would not be pleased with this raucous version of piano music being played on their grand piano. However, when the tempo slowed to George Gershwin's *Rhapsody in Blue*, Sarah realized where Jake was going with this.

The music came to an end. Jake looked at Gracie then at Gordon. "What does a man have to do to earn a cup of coffee around here?"

Gracie started to laugh. "Wow, Jake. What do you mean you're not accomplished? It must have taken you hours and hours of practice to become this good."

"It did, young lady. Hours and hours."

"Didn't you hate it?"

"I would have rather been outside playing road hockey with my friends, that's for sure."

"But you and your friends must have had fun playing that kind of music together."

"That didn't come until years later. Once I got through some classical stuff and learned how to appreciate and write music, then the fun came. Without the basic training, I never would have learned the fun stuff."

Gracie looked at Jake with a new respect. "Can you teach me some of the fun stuff?"

"Will you continue to practice the classical stuff if I do?"

"That's blackmail."

"It's more like compromise."

"Can I think about it?"

"You sure can. You might want to talk to your daddy and grandmama about it too."

Sarah interrupted. "Maybe it's time we fed this man. He just got off a plane and hasn't eaten in hours."

"I'm sorry, Jake. I forgot you've been in airports and on a plane since breakfast time. Grandma and I prepared some food before you got here. Come into the kitchen and eat."

Jake put his things away in the guest room before he sat down to a cold buffet. He declined a cold drink in favour of a cup of coffee while they caught up on all the news and events since their last time together.

Later in the evening, while Gordon and Gracie gave the kitchen a good wipe down, Sarah and Jake had a short time alone in the living room.

"It was nice of you to accept Gracie's invitation to join us for the weekend."

"I was deeply touched when she called me." He fiddled with the cuff on his sweater. "I miss my grandchildren and when Gracie called ... I ... Well, I just felt wanted, needed maybe." He turned to Sarah. "I hope you didn't mind when I accepted. I know you worry about me intruding into your life too much."

"Mind? Nothing of the sort, Jake. You're a good friend and you've been so kind to Gracie. It was her idea for you to come and I'm glad she thought of it." She looked around the spacious apartment. "It's going to be hard for her to say goodbye to this place and I think you being here is going to make it a little easier for her, especially since you can plan your next fishing trip after she moves to her new home in Canada. It will give her one more thing to look forward to."

She took his hand in hers and kissed it. "Besides I really am happy to see you again."

Chapter Twenty

The weekend went well if one didn't count the number of increasingly strained conversations between Gordon and his in-laws. They wanted visiting privileges once a month which meant Gracie would have to travel to stay with them. Gordon argued that whatever Gracie's schedule would end up being, considering getting her into the sports she wanted, he could not commit to that arrangement.

"I think she should not make any plans to travel back here until at least the end of summer. She needs that time to become accustomed to living in Montreal, making new friends, developing a relationship with teammates and new coaches and trainers, not even to mention getting over any homesickness she might suffer from. A clean break might give her time to adjust to her new environment." When he stopped for a breath, he sensed an argument coming from his mother-in-law, so he quickly continued. "She's at a vulnerable age and it will be hard enough without uprooting her every month to bring her here, where there may be sad memories for her."

"She will have good memories of this place. We've had many happy years together here. Gracie always enjoyed her time with us." It was George who spoke up. "We've been a major part of her life since she was hardly more than a toddler. You can't just up and take her away from us. You … you just can't do this." His voice was breaking as he finished.

As he explained to his mother later, Gordon had been trying hard to control his temper. He had hoped it wouldn't come to this. He knew exactly how his father-in-law felt. He had felt the same when his daughter was taken from him and moved across an international border to be raised in a strange city when she was only four years old. He almost reminded the older man of that but fought to maintain his cool and not say anything that he might regret. He had always gotten along well with George and Elizabeth and he wanted that relationship to continue.

"Once we've moved and I can see that Gracie is settling in well, we can discuss this again. It might work if you were to consider coming to Montreal to visit so that she's not disrupted." He felt this plan might work out better for his daughter, at least for the first while.

Elizabeth's lip curled up at one end and she turned her back on Gordon as she spoke. "I feel this is the beginning of the end. She won't be allowed to come here and before long there'll be excuses why it's not a good time for us to come there. We'll become strangers to her."

"That's not fair, Elizabeth." He was fighting hard not to raise his voice. "I have no intention of keeping you from your granddaughter. I know how much Gracie loves the two of you. Both of you have been very kind to her and to me. Believe me when I say I know how hard it is to be separated by three hundred and fifty miles and an international border from someone you love dearly. I've had to live with that arrangement for the past eight years. I …" He stopped mid-sentence and looked from one to the other. "Let's finish this later." He ran his hand through his hair, tried to smile and backed out of the room.

♥♥♥

Later that afternoon, before Gordon had had an opportunity to tell his mother about the incident with his in-laws, Elizabeth and Sarah were preparing vegetables for dinner when Elizabeth tried to get Sarah's opinion on the matter of visitation rights. Sarah, unaware of the conversation that had taken place earlier, was not prepared for the question.

"What do you mean 'visitation rights'?"

"George and I feel that Gracie should be allowed to spend one weekend a month with us. She has friends here that she'll miss and familiar places she'll want to see. New York is her home. Two days out of every thirty shouldn't be too much to ask for. As a grandparent, surely you would agree?"

Sarah put down the potato she was peeling. "Have you had a discussion about this with Gordon and Gracie?"

"Yes, as a matter of fact, we have."

"And how do they feel about it?"

"Gordon is against it and Gracie has been stalling with her answer. Poor child. She probably doesn't want to hurt her father's feelings."

"Or maybe she doesn't want to her hurt yours."

Before Elizabeth could respond, Sarah had picked up the peeler and was attacking the potato with it. "I don't think this is a conversation for you and I to have. This decision is not one for me to make or even argue for or against. This probably is one that shouldn't even be made at this point. No one knows how Gracie might feel after a month in Montreal. She may be ready for a visit back to New York or she may need more time to adjust to her new home before being able to resurrect the memories here."

"Would you feel the same way if it was you?"

"It *was* me eight years ago. The grandchild I loved and saw often was taken from her home near me and moved to a foreign country. I have not been allowed to see her more than a few times a year. I know exactly how you are feeling. However, it's not how you or I feel, it's how Gracie feels that matters and the poor child won't know how she's feeling until she's been in her new home for a while."

"I should have known you would side with your son. You've never forgiven my daughter for trying to make a better life for her child here."

"Let's not go there." Sarah put the potato and paring knife down. "I'll let you finish fixing dinner while I go to my room and sew a new zipper into my mouth. I've about chewed this one through."

Chapter Twenty-one

Dinner that evening was subdued to say the least. Gordon and his daughter's grandparents agreed to reassess the visiting privileges at a later date. He had already confided to his mother that he was concerned the Chalmers might take court action to gain their "rights" and he didn't want Gracie involved in a court battle on top of everything else going on in her life. Everyone tried to be polite and kept the conversation light for Gracie's sake.

Sarah wished that she had left the evening before when Jake had, but she had opted to stay an extra day not knowing there was a storm brewing among in-laws. Gracie made Jake promise that he was serious about coming to Canada for a fishing trip in the early summer. It appeared to Sarah that the child was more concerned about seeing him again than she was about her own grandparents. *Maybe it's because he doesn't give her grief about anything. He just enjoys her and she him with no strings attached.*

She left the next day at noon while Gracie was at school. She had received a manicure the evening before from her granddaughter who had also chosen the outfit her grandmother was to wear on the plane ride home. "You have such nice clothes, Grandma." She held up matching denim pants and topper and a T-shirt the colour of Sarah's pale blue eyes. "These will be comfortable I think and they'll go with your big navy blue bag. I like that you wear denim pants and stuff. You don't dress like an old lady."

Sarah had smiled at the intended compliment. Children can be so honest, so she was happy that her stylish wardrobe met with her granddaughter's approval. Heaven forbid she look like an old lady. Lord knows she did her best — weekly gym workouts, monthly spa treatments and facials, daily walks and regular root touch-ups. She drew the line at any body enhancements but did her best to keep it looking healthy and firm. She was coming close to that senior citizen age of sixty-five but had no intention of retiring from any of her activities yet.

By the time she arrived back home, the snow had gone and Ottawa was feeling a little more spring-like. April can be such a dirty month with the snow melting and leaving behind winter's residue. It usually would take a couple of weeks with no snow to feel the spring air's warmth and the ground to dry up and make walking more pleasant. Temperatures in the high teens were being forecast for the rest of the week so her spirits were high a few days later as she walked toward the market to pick up cheese and homemade sausage from one of the vendors. In a few weeks these streets would fill with people enjoying the street cafes and vendors displaying their wares outside. Pop-up tables filled with artists, writers and crafters would soon be adding to the colour and carnival atmosphere of the Byward Market. The many parks surrounding Parliament Hill and the downtown area would be awash with tulips and tourists would soon be arriving to celebrate spring in the nation's capital.

A man brushed her arm as he hurried along the sidewalk ahead of her. She noticed the dishevelled clothes as he passed but it wasn't until he had disappeared into a doorway that she realized he had shuffled along the walkway with the same slight limp as the man who had slept in her doorway a few months back. She sped up to try to catch another glimpse of him but someone rolling out a rack with dozens of handbags and scarves hanging from it blocked her way. By the time she made her way around it there was no one resembling him on the street. After looking into several retail outlets, she knew he had disappeared into a doorway somewhere along the way.

Could he have been the same person? If so, he was probably living somewhere nearby. There were a couple of men's shelters in the area so she decided to keep an eye out for him on her future ventures into the market. It still nagged at her conscience how she had brushed him off in the freezing temperatures that night. She thought about the shelters and wondered how they had fared this past winter. It had been a record breaker for cold temperatures and it must have been difficult to keep all those homeless people warm and fed. *Maybe they can use a volunteer.*

A block from her condo building she ran into Olivia who was on her way back from a dentist appointment.

"Are you out enjoying the warm spring day?"

"I picked up some sausage and cheese for our bridge game tomorrow. It's my turn and I haven't stocked my refrigerator since I came home. You ladies will have to be satisfied with a deli lunch. I promise to make fresh buns to have with them."

"Sarah, you always have a way of making a cold buffet seem like a gourmet smorgasbord. I doubt we'll be disappointed."

"You know, while I was in the market I could have sworn I saw that poor homeless man I booted out of our doorway last winter. I tried to catch him but he disappeared."

"And what would you do with him if you caught him?"

"I don't know. Apologize for one thing, I guess. I hate that I was so callous. I would try to make it up to him by buying him a hot meal in the market."

"He's probably forgotten all about the incident. I'm sure you're not the only person that has ignored him on the streets. They're probably used to it and more surprised by the people who do give them something."

"Well, I haven't forgotten even if he has. I'll watch for him and try to make it up to him."

Olivia shook her head and smiled at her friend. "You do so much for so many people, Sarah. You can't feed and house them all. I admire your kind and generous nature."

"If I could, I would."

"Would what?"

"Feed and house them all. When I see them having to beg just to eat each day, I feel guilty that I come home and have a full fridge and pantry. I want to put it all in a shopping cart and wheel it out and share it with them."

The elevator stopped at Olivia's floor. She gave Sarah a hug and said, "You're one of the good ones, my friend. I'll see you tomorrow."

Sarah lingered as she put her purchases in her fridge. She eyed the left-over partial stuffed salmon and the white wine she had cooling on a shelf to have with the fish later. *Why am I so blessed? It doesn't seem fair.*

Chapter Twenty-two

"I guess Junior will be happy to see the end of the school year so he can get Gracie settled in Montreal and not have to travel back and forth to New York every week." Olivia sorted the cards in her hand as she spoke.

Olivia was one of very few people who referred to Sarah's son as Junior. It was what Sarah and his father, Gordon Senior, had called him in his younger days. Since he had become a successful businessman and known to almost everyone by his given name, everyone used Gordon or Gordie when speaking to or about him. Every once in a while, just out of habit, she'd call him Junior and for some reason, Olivia had picked up on it. He didn't seem to mind. At least he had never mentioned it.

"All of us will be happy to have something close to normal restored in our lives once again. Gracie and Gordon will have a lot of adjustments to work through but at least they'll have the summer to sort through everything before she starts a new school and a new country's curriculum in September."

Margaret understood fully how suddenly families' lives can be turned around by calamity. She covered Sarah's hand with her own. "It's amazing how resilient young people can be. They usually adjust better than we can. I'm sure Gracie will make a few new friends through her sports activities over the next few months and will look at school as a new adventure. Usually by the time September rolls around children are already bored with too much time on their hands and look forward to a little more structure. She's a pretty outgoing young lady and I can't imagine her not being accepted by her classmates."

"I hope you're right, Margaret. She's been through so much but she does seem to accept whatever is placed in front of her. I think fishing and boating and getting back into track and field will keep her occupied. She sure is looking forward to her first fishing venture with her father and Jake."

"You know, Gerald was quite a fisherman in his day. Growing up in the Sault Ste. Marie area, most weekends involved camping or fishing of some sort. There were so many lakes, rivers and beaches within a two-hundred-mile radius that I think every lad knew how to handle a motor boat and fishing rod before they were out of elementary school. He might enjoy taking Gordon and Sarah out on the Ottawa or Mississippi River when they're in town." Helen added. "In fact, I *know* he would enjoy it."

"That would be fun for Gordon too, I think. He hasn't had much experience with camping and fishing so I'm sure he'd welcome the help of any and all experienced pseudo-grandfathers willing to do so."

❣ ❣ ❣

April progressed into May and the weather was promising to be unseasonably warm for the Victoria Day long weekend. Gordon had been busy getting all the paperwork done for the rental of the apartment in New York. On the advice of his lawyer, he had decided not to sell it. The rental market for high end apartments in that city was showing a definite need for units such as theirs. They arranged for a property management firm to handle short term rentals for the time being. This would give him a grace period to help his daughter understand that her home would be in Montreal now but still allow her the comfort of New York still being part of her life. He also knew there was a real possibility that as an adult she may wish to move back there, or even go to university there, something that would make her maternal grandmother happy. Better she have a home she owned if that happened than to be a victim of New York's high real estate and rental prices.

Gracie appeared to be accepting the move to Canada readily enough. Sarah knew the two of them had checked out and applied to have her enrolled in a track program that had produced a couple of highly ranked competitive athletes.

❣❣❣

"Grandma, do you know that there are about one hundred and eighteen different species of freshwater fish in Quebec? Jake told me that most Canadians like walleyes the best and the fishing season for them will be open before the end of May. I can hardly wait to get there and go fishing. Do you think you'll be able to come with us? I hope my dad can get a boat so we can go soon after I move there."

Sarah laughed silently at the enthusiasm her granddaughter was displaying. Obviously, she was staying in touch with Jake, the expert fisherman. Her heart sang at the thought of Gracie showing such joy at the thought of moving. She had been afraid of the opposite. She was positive that Jake had not known the door he was opening when he had taken this young girl on her first boat ride and fishing expedition in Florida. No one had known. No one had foreseen the tragedy that was about to change all of their lives.

Of course Gracie's enthusiasm could be a cover up for how she may truly feel. It could be her own defence mechanism against fear of an unknown future. It must be extremely hard on the young teenager being pulled from one family to another. The Chalmers family was close knit and loved her very much, cherished her really. They had been a solid, strong unit. Now she was facing life with her single father and a single grandmother who lived in separate cities. She must be aware of the tension between her father and her maternal grandparents. She hadn't attended Gracie's thirteenth birthday, allowing her maternal grandparents full privileges for probably the last birthday she would celebrate in New York. Was the young girl feeling a sense of being pulled in two directions? Maybe that was the reason she felt drawn to Jake. Maybe, to her, he was a grandfather-figure who was completely neutral. He cared for the child unconditionally. It didn't matter to him who she belonged to or where she lived. He had promised he would stay in touch no matter where she was, no strings attached. He only cared about making her happy — the way a grandparent should care.

When her call with Gracie ended, Sarah picked up the phone and keyed in Jake's number. She received his voicemail and left a message. Within a half hour her phone rang.

"Hello?"

"Hi, darlin'. Sorry I missed your call."

"So am I. I like hearing you call me darlin' when I call." She felt a tug in her chest when she realized her words were true. "So I hear you've been giving my granddaughter the whole scoop on fishing in Quebec. I hope she hasn't been pestering you about it."

His warm laughter set her at ease. "That little girl is about as enthusiastic a fisherwoman as I've ever met. I just hope Quebec waterways are going to provide her with all the fish she's hoping to catch. She's been doing her own reading and research and knows more about fishing up there than I do. All I'll have to do is show her how to bait a hook and reel them in."

"So have you set a date to come up?"

"Fishing is always better early in the season than it is in the dead of summer so I'm hoping we might plan something for mid to late June. I guess it all depends when they make their move up there and get settled in."

"Are you still planning on making a stop in Ottawa?"

"I'm thinking that's where I'll fly into and out of."

"So you're going to fly? I thought you might drive."

"I'll rent a car in Ottawa to go to Montreal." He hesitated. "Or we could drive there together in your car."

"That's possible, I guess. Will you stay here for a few days?"

"I'll stay for as long as you'll have me. I'd like to see some of your home town, maybe get to meet the rest of those ladies you play cards with."

"Well, they sure want to meet you, Jake. You already know Olivia and Margaret, but I'll throw a dinner party for you to meet Helen and Stella and a couple of spouses. I'm looking forward to it."

"Are you, darlin'? I sometimes feel you'd rather keep our friendship long distance."

He caught her off guard. Of course that's how it would appear to him. She actually *had* wanted to keep him at a distance. He was a man it would be easy to fall in love with. To get real comfortable with. Two good men had left her mourning their absence, and she did not want to put herself through anything like that again. It would be hard enough losing a friend but to lose another love would be devastating. Keeping him at a distance was her way of protecting herself. If he became a permanent year-round fixture in her life and anything were to happen to him, well …

"Our time together was shorter than usual this past winter. I wasn't with you long enough for you to get under my skin. Besides, someone needs to cook a few healthy meals for you from time to time. Those fast foods you eat are going to be the death of you."

"What are you talking about? Pizza is full of vegetables. And when I'm at home I barbecue."

"I am picturing racks of ribs and twelve-ounce beef steaks on your grill, Jakub Tatarek."

"Ya got me, sweetheart! Guilty as hell."

They agreed on him coming up several days before the fishing weekend in Montreal sometime in June. Sarah hung up the phone and gazed out her living room window. *What are you doing to yourself, girl? You vowed never to do this again.*

Chapter Twenty-three

"So Jake's arriving on Monday?" Helen met up with Sarah at the mailboxes downstairs.

"Yes. I'll figure out a day to have all of you for dinner. He wants to meet all my friends."

"And we all want to meet him. He sounds like a nice man."

"He is. I think he and Gerald have similar personalities."

"And Gracie? Is she coming here also?"

"No, Gracie has tryouts for a track meet coming up in Montreal but she's counting the days to next weekend. She's been marking them off on the calendar and checking the fishing almanacs and moon phases figuring out the best days for fishing. I didn't realize fishing was so scientific. I always thought you pick a sunny day, grab your fishing rod and find a body of water. Little did I know." She rolled her eyes as she moved to the door.

Sarah stepped outside and strolled toward the market. She didn't like shopping on Saturdays as there were usually lines of people at each vendor but she wanted to get her groceries today so she could concentrate on getting the guest room ready tomorrow for Jake's arrival the next day. The day was cloudy with the threat of rain so she was happy to see there were fewer shoppers out on the streets. It was still early in the season but the market had an abundance of fresh local greens: several types of lettuce, young green onions, radishes, and baby carrots. Asparagus was also a great spring vegetable. She found several booths selling fresh strawberries as well. She stopped at her favourite bakery and cheese stores and headed back home. She always ordered her meat from a local butcher whom she trusted to deliver the best cuts of meat.

Well, Jake, I hope your stomach enjoys the healthy meals you are going to be eating over the next week or so.

She hummed along to the music on her favourite music station. She loved the pieces from the '70s they usually played on Sunday mornings. Giving the quilt on the bed a final smoothing, she stood back, pleased with the effect a few changes had made to the décor of the guest room. It looked a little more gender neutral. The room was painted in pale pastels and had always presented a feminine aura. A few peacock-blue and mustard-coloured accessories gave just enough sharp contrast to change the personality of the room from delicate to vibrant. *Vibrant, just like you, Jake.*

Guest room done, she turned her thoughts to baking. Maybe a flan with the fresh strawberries and kiwi. She could make the cake pastry and the cream filling today and add the fruit and glaze tomorrow. Having made desserts for a living in an earlier life, she was always prepared and knew each step in the various processes — what could be made ahead and what needed to be done last minute.

By the time she lifted the covers to get into bed, she had the first two stages of the flan done and a rhubarb crumble in the refrigerator. *Enough to satisfy his sweet tooth for a couple of days.*

When the alarm rang at 6:45 a.m. she was already in the shower. Jake's plane was arriving just past noon but she still had work to do. With a towel wrapped around her head Sarah sliced the fruit and made the glaze for the flan. She also removed chicken thighs from the freezer and boiled potatoes and eggs for potato salad. It was mid-morning before she got around to doing her hair and make-up. The traffic to the airport wouldn't be too bad for a daytime flight so she knew she had plenty of time to pamper herself a little.

She had told Jake she would park the car and meet him inside the terminal. When his flight arrival was announced, she was surprised by the flutter in her stomach. *It's only Jake.* She sat on a bench near the luggage retrieval area and after what seemed like an unreasonable wait, she finally spotted him coming down the escalator. His broad grin when he saw her seemed to brighten the whole airport. A woman who she guessed to be in her late fifties was talking animatedly to him on the ride down. When he waved at Sarah, the woman sent her a hard stare.

What the …?

"Hi darlin'." Two strong arms wrapped her in an embrace and his lips found hers.

When Sarah stepped back, the woman was right behind Jake and appeared to be waiting for him. Sarah raised an eyebrow in question. Jake flushed and tried move her away from the woman. Sarah noticed the woman reach out and place a hand on his arm.

"Aren't you forgetting something?" she asked.

Who was this woman and what did she want? Jake removed the woman's hand and said in a polite tone, "No. I am not. Now I have to get my luggage and not keep this sweet lady waiting any longer."

"But … your number?"

"It was really nice chatting with you on the plane." Jake placed a hand behind Sarah's elbow and motioned to the luggage carousel. "I see my bags going around the gizmo now. Let's get them and get out of this crowd." He pressed Sarah to move with him and didn't allow the woman the opportunity for a reply.

As he grabbed his bags, he whispered to Sarah to move quickly. Bewildered, she turned and headed toward the door leading to the parking garage.

"I was going to offer to bring the car around to the door so you don't have to haul your luggage into the parking lot."

"Don't you dare leave me where that woman can pester me."

Sarah was confused. Jake seemed pleased that her car was in one of the rows on the closer side of the garage. They loaded his bags into the back of her SUV and settled into the comfortable seats inside.

"So, what in the world was that all about? I was beginning to think you brought a girlfriend with you and had forgotten to tell me."

"If I didn't already know *you*, I would wonder if all women from Ottawa were a wee bit weird and a whole lot bossy." He slid his seatbelt into place and secured it before he turned to her, a twinkle in his eye. "Is there such a shortage of men up here that women just nab any one they meet?"

"Why, Jakub Tatarek! She was hitting on you!" Sarah burst into laughter.

"I don't think it's that funny. Are you suggesting women don't find me attractive?"

"That's not it at all. For heaven's sake, what happened?"

"She had the seat next to mine and seemed pleasant at first. We chatted about where we're from and where we're going. Turns out she's from Ottawa and just had a job transfer to Chicago. She went to find a place to live and get some orientation at her workplace. When she found out I was single she became a little more aggressive in her approach. She thought it was fate that sat her beside someone who could become her first friend in her new home. She wanted to know what part of Chicago I live in, where I work, what I like to do in my leisure time. She suggested we could hook up when she goes back and I could help her get acquainted with everything in and around Chicago. She wanted us to exchange phone numbers so we can keep in touch and get to know each other better. I told her I was coming to stay with a dear friend in Canada and didn't know how long I'd be here. She didn't seem to get the message. I tried being polite but you saw how she clung to me. I wish there was some way I could find out what flight she's going to be on going back so I could pick a different one."

"I'm surprised she didn't give you that information." Sarah put hand on Jake's arm. "Don't worry, I'll protect you from that bad woman." Another bout of laughter brought on a burst from him too.

"I guess I sound like a sissy but I've never been hit on so aggressively before. I don't like being rude to anyone but I didn't know how to deal with her." He squared his shoulders, sat a little straighter in his seat and looked in his visor mirror. "Guess this old guy still has it."

"I better get you out of here before the seatbelt snaps from the pressure of that swelled chest."

They hadn't gone too far along the parkway before Jake's cell phone rang.

"Do you want me to screen that call for you?" Sarah couldn't pass up the opportunity to tease him.

"Actually, it's from another female who finds me kinda likeable." He put the phone to his ear. "Hiya, Gracie. Got all your fishing gear ready?"

Chapter Twenty-four

Jake pushed his chair away from the table. After giving him just a light meal on his arrival, Sarah had served him a more hardy meal at suppertime. "I don't know how you do it but you sure have a way of making my stomach happy and my arteries grateful at the same time. You should write a cookbook on how to cook healthy and happy meals. I know that everything you cook for me is heart healthy yet my tummy says 'thank you for the great treat.'"

"There are enough healthy eating cookbooks out there, the public doesn't need another but I'm happy you enjoy my cooking. Maybe I should give your new friend some of my recipes."

"New friend?"

"The lady who's going to be your new best friend in Chicago." Before Jake could respond, there was a knock on Sarah's door. When she opened it, Helen and Gerald were in the hallway.

"I could smell your cooking all the way down the elevator shaft." Gerald was grinning.

"I think the only guy with an appetite to equal yours is sitting in my dining room. Come in and meet Jake." She made the introductions and offered dessert and coffee to her friends.

The two men shook hands and immediately became engaged in a conversation about the NFL trades currently taking place.

Sarah left Helen to listen to the pros and cons of which players should be protected and which should not while she plated two pieces of her fruit flan for the new guests. Sarah enjoyed watching NFL games so she was able to inject her opinions into the conversation but Helen had no interest whatsoever. After an hour of football talk, the conversation got around to fishing. That was something Helen knew quite a bit about but it was lost on Sarah. It seemed the men were experts on both topics.

"I like your friends." Jake closed the door after the couple left. "Gerald is my kind of guy."

"That's nice to hear. It didn't seem like the two of you could find common ground." Sarah smiled as Jake emptied the last of the coffee into his mug. She was glad to see him making himself at home.

Jake smiled back. "He grew up living in a city on the Great Lakes just like I did. Both are hockey towns surrounded by fishing. We mutually know all about cold winters with lots of snow and how important industry is to the economy."

"Helen and Gerald were childhood sweethearts who were separated by distance and careers after high school. They were reunited only a couple of years ago when Gerald retired and moved to Ottawa to live closer to his son. They ran into each other downstairs in the lobby and the rest, as they say, is history. Both of their spouses had died and they were grateful to find each other. Theirs is a love story with a happy ending."

"All love stories should have happy endings." He squeezed her shoulder. "I'm going to turn in, darlin'. I had to be at the airport early since it was an international flight. Do you have anything special on the agenda tomorrow?"

"I didn't make any definite plans for us except for a little dinner party on Wednesday evening. I thought we might do the tourist thingy tomorrow. Being the capital of Canada, our city offers several great tour packages. I thought I'd leave the car in the parking garage and maybe we can take a tour or two. The guides on the buses and boats can tell you so much more than I can about our city's history. Maybe we can lunch at one of the bistros in the Market."

"Sounds wonderful. We can just sit back and relax, maybe hold hands while someone else does the driving and the talking." He kissed her lightly. "I'm looking forward to my few days here in your city, your home."

"I'm glad you're here." She kissed him back. "Goodnight, Jake. I'll have the coffee on early in the morning. I know you're an early riser."

♥♥♥

Just before seven o'clock the next morning, Sarah could hear Jake running the water in the shower. She turned the coffeemaker on and placed a loaf of rye bread from the bakery shop on the counter near the toaster. A short while later, she thought she heard a soft knock on her condo door. When she opened it to see who was knocking at that hour of the morning, she heard the elevator door close and there was a kitchen-towel-wrapped parcel on the floor in front of her. She scooped it up and was surrounded by the aroma of fresh-baked bread wafting from inside the towel. She knew immediately who had left the gift.

"Good morning, sweetheart." A clean-shaven cheek was pressed next to hers and a large palm closed around her shoulder. "Mmm mmm, are those fresh-baked buns I see on the table?"

"Yes. My friend a couple floors down delivered them bright and early this morning."

"Anyone who gets up at dawn to bake fresh bread for a neighbour has to be one special friend."

"Her name is Stella and she is famous for her buns — the edible kind."

"Did she just drop them off and run?"

"Yes. She did include a note welcoming you to Ottawa."

Stella handed a little note card to Jake.

She didn't tell him that at one time Stella's buns had almost caused a breakup between Gerald and Helen. That was their story to tell but it had caused enough of a ruckus to almost bring Sarah home early from Florida. It had all worked out well in the end with the two women becoming close friends and Stella buying Helen's employment agency from her when she retired.

"How are the buns?" She watched Jake slather marmalade on his third one.

"That's one of those questions that doesn't have a right answer."

"How so?"

"If I tell you they're the best buns I've ever eaten, you may not speak to me again but if said otherwise, I'd be doing that kind lady, Stella, an injustice."

Sarah patted his shoulder. "You're safe. I like your honesty, Jake. They are the best that anyone could ever eat. I pride myself on my cooking but even I know when I've been bested — in the baking department anyway."

"I hope I get to thank your friend in person for her kindness."

"You will. She's invited to come for dinner with the others on Wednesday. I hope she'll come."

Jake used his napkin to wipe marmalade from his chin and stood. "Are we gonna sit and eat all morning or are we gonna hop on a bus and take a look around the city?"

"I'll put these things in the dishwasher and we'll be on our way."

♥ ♥ ♥

They took a tour bus that allowed them to get on and off at various sites as many times as they chose to do so. They saw the war museum, the parliament buildings from the outside since the building was undergoing a major renovation that would take many years to complete. Then got back on a bus for a ride to the farm where the horses were trained for the Royal Canadian Mounted Police musical ride. It was early afternoon when they stopped for lunch in the Byward Market. After hours of sitting in the open upper level of the tour bus, it was a treat to sit in the quiet shade of the restaurant patio and watch the passersby going about their business. Ottawa was truly a city of varied ethnicities and in tourist season even more variations of dress and language were abundant in the popular market.

Jake, being Jake, carried on conversations with many of the people who caught his eye. He loved the buskers even though Chicago had more than their share. Some from across the river were entertaining the crowds in their native French both in song and poetry. He insisted on buying one of the ever-popular beavertails, a pastry famous in the market. Unbeknownst to him, Sarah took a picture of him trying to strike up a conversation with a French-speaking toddler who was waving a Canadian flag and holding a stuffed moose. She decided she'd have it framed as a souvenir of his first visit to the market.

It warmed her heart to see him having so much fun. She had always known he was an easy-going, pleasant man who always found joy in simple pleasures around him. Today she realized the joy he brought not only to her but to everyone around him. He was leaving everyone with smiles on their faces. He radiated goodness.

Suddenly she felt a sensation of being watched. Not an unpleasant feeling, just a feeling. She glanced around and her eyes fell on a man leaning against the wall of one of the businesses across the square. He was dressed in T-shirt and shorts, sandals on his feet. He appeared to be looking directly at her but with no indication of recognition or wanting to get her attention. He was in the shade of an awning so she was unable to make out any of his features. After a minute or so of staring, he straightened his stance and turned, walking away with a familiar slight limp. It hit her in the gut. She knew exactly who he was and stood up to try to catch him. Just then Jake took her arm.

"Sorry, darling', I got so taken with that little fellow I … Is something wrong?"

"I have to catch that man." She started across the square.

"Sarah, what's wrong? Did he take something from you?" Jake caught up to her and was matching her fast stride.

"No. He … I … Damn! He's gone." She had lost sight of him again.

Chapter Twenty-five

"Let me get this straight. This guy is a homeless person that was sleeping in your entryway last winter. You disturbed him and he ran away and you feel guilty because you didn't give him food or a bed?"

"I feel guilty because I actually kicked him. No wonder he ran away. Jake, it was the coldest night of the winter. I didn't even offer him money to buy a hot cup of coffee or a bowl of soup." Sarah wrung her hands together as she paced the living room floor. "Obviously he's still on the street. He looked cleaner and neater, that's why I didn't recognize him right away but he's still hanging around the market."

"Sarah, sweetheart, we spent a half hour searching those streets and didn't find him. I think you did all you could." He took her by her shoulders and crouched slightly so that their eyes were level. "You can't beat yourself up over this. What's done is done. You could give a donation to a shelter in that neighbourhood and hope that he or someone like him benefits from it."

"I have, Jake. I even volunteer once a week at one of the soup kitchens in the hope he'll walk in one day and I can apologize."

"You seem obsessed. Does he look familiar? Do you think you might know him?"

"No. I don't know why I feel the way I do. His eyes, or at least the eye that wasn't hidden by his blanket, was so full of sadness. He looked so forlorn, so lost. It was almost as if he was meant to be here. Right here on my doorstep."

"I don't know what to tell you, darlin'. If you like, we can go back tonight and have a drink on a patio and see if he comes by again."

"Jake, I can't ask you to spend your vacation helping me find a homeless man who may already be begging or finding shelter in another part of the city. I …" She looked at him. "You are one of the kindest people I know. If you feel I've done all I can then I guess I should listen to you."

He took her in his arms and held her in a tender embrace. "You're being harder on yourself than you deserve. I know you do more than your share for so many charities. You are not going to be banished to hell because you overlooked one person out of the thousands that you have helped. Put it behind you, Sarah. Obviously he feels no ill will toward you or he would have approached you."

She nodded in acceptance of his advice and kissed him on the cheek.

The next morning, she had him stuffing crepes with a seafood mixture and wrapping them tightly. She would slice them into bite-sized pieces for one of the appetizers before dinner. Gerald rang the doorbell a couple hours later inviting Jake to join him and a couple buddies at the golf course.

"We all know when Sarah throws a dinner party it's an all-day operation. She probably won't even notice that you're gone until it's time to seat you at the table. Helen will be up shortly to give her a hand if she needs or even wants one."

"I feel guilty leaving her to fix it all by herself when I'm the reason she's doing it."

"Believe me when I tell you, she won't mind me taking you away for a few hours. When these women prepare for an event, they don't want anyone, especially a man, getting between them and the food. Come on, we have lots of time to get eighteen holes in before you're even missed."

Gerald was right. Helen did arrive and helped prepare the appetizers. By the time Jake arrived back at the condo, the dining room table was magnificently set with Sarah's best china, sterling flatware and crystal. He moaned when he saw it.

"You don't look pleased." Sarah was surprised by his reaction.

"Everything looks amazing. I'm moaning because I know all this fancy stuff doesn't go in the dishwasher. Does this mean we will be up until two o'clock in the morning washing it all by hand?" He took her hand and kissed it. "These hands of yours have already been put through hours and hours of work today."

Chapter Twenty-six

"I don't know who will be sorrier to see Jake leave when he goes back to Chicago, you or Gerald." Helen picked up her hand and arranged her cards.

It was Friday and Jake and Gerald had gone golfing while the girls played cards at Helen's and Gerald's condo. Sarah and Jake planned on leaving the next morning for Montreal.

"You've forgotten about Gracie." Sarah was sorting her hand trying to keep from frowning at the lack of face cards. "She has phoned every day with weather and fish-biting forecasts after googling the appropriate apps for all the latest info. She doesn't even call on my phone anymore. She calls directly to her fishing guide and new best friend."

"Why wouldn't she be taken with him? Jake is such a gentle, kind, likable guy. The kind of grandpa every child should have." Margaret made her opening bid.

"He's very easy on the eyes as well. You didn't mention that he's sexy as hell, Sarah."

Startled by Helen's comment, Sarah smiled. "I didn't realize he was. Jake has always been Jake. A good friend and a great guy to go out to dinner and occasionally dancing with. We like to watch sports on TV and he enjoys my cooking. He's never been more to me than that."

"You mean you haven't noticed how he can't keep his eyes off you? Anyone can see he adores you." Helen paused after she completed the first round of bidding. "You don't mean to tell me you guys were on the road together for several days, sharing motel rooms and you know nothing about his sexiness?"

"It's not like that. Jake and I are friends. That's it."

"You two do more hugging and kissing and smiling and looking and touching than any two friends I've ever seen."

Sarah was about to comment back but noticed all three women were looking at her as if daring her to deny it. "Well, I … We … That is … Damn it! You don't think Jake thinks of us as more than friends. Do you?"

All started to speak at once. It was Olivia, who had been silent until then, who got to finish her response. "I think Jake has hoped you were more than friends for a few years now. It's you who has kept him at bay with your friendly but 'companionable' maneuvering of your relationship. I'm surprised he hasn't 'declared himself' by now to use an old-fashioned phrase. I'm even more surprised that you haven't noticed the love and desire in his eyes."

"Love and desire? Jake?" Sarah sat back in her chair. "He's never given me any indication of wanting more than friendship."

"His eyes are telling you every time he looks at you. You are blind, Sarah."

Sarah stared at her cards then laid them face down on the table. "This ruins everything." She stood and walked to the window. "I don't want another relationship. After a terrible divorce from one man and two gut-wrenching funerals for two wonderful, loving men, I swore I would never ever allow myself to become involved with a fourth. I cannot do this again. I cannot do it to myself and I cannot do it to Jake."

She turned and looked at each of her friends. "Why can't people just be friends? Like us — we four? We love, hug and care for each other. Why couldn't it just stay like that between Jake and me? And now there's Gracie. Gracie. My God there's Gracie. I can't pull him out of her life. What am I going to do?"

The others put their cards down. Helen moved to Sarah and put an arm around her waist then guided her to the sofa in the living room. "Sarah, I see you looking at Jake the same way he looks at you. If you were honest with yourself, I think you would have to agree that your feelings for him are deeper than you think. You care for this man. Admit it."

Olivia sank into the armchair closest to the sofa. "I've been going to Florida and spending time with you and Jake down there for quite a few years. I know how your friendship started and grew. I used to envy you, that you could have a normal friendship with a man and not have anyone question it. It seemed so casual and natural." She leaned over and took one her friend's hands in hers. "It's not Jake's fault that he developed deeper feelings over the years. It's not your fault either. It just happened. When you said you were travelling back together, I honestly thought you and he had come to terms with your deepening relationship. Then all hell broke loose and all of a sudden you were needed in your son's and Gracie's lives. Nothing has been normal since, especially with Jake and Gracie's budding friendship. Now you are caught in a vortex of everyone's emotions, emotions that you can't control."

Sarah looked up. Her friends were nodding in unison.

"What am I going to do? I don't want to give Jake the wrong signals."

"Maybe you're not." Margaret smiled at her. "Maybe the signals you're giving are the right ones and you just don't know it yet."

"You don't understand. I cannot survive another husband. I refuse to. I just couldn't say goodbye to another good man."

"Then don't. Nothing says you have to marry him. And if you do, then just give him the best damn care you can so you are the first to go." Olivia squeezed her hand.

"Then what am I to do?"

"Ride the wave. Enjoy this man who wants to make you happy. You don't know how lucky you are. Let him be a part of your life. Nothing says he has to be your whole life, just a part of it. Something tells me he would be very happy with that. You do like him, don't you?"

"Yes. Very much."

"Then why send him away if you're happier with him than without him? And by the way, Helen is right, he is sexy as hell." Olivia winked as she let go of Sarah's hand. "Now let's get back to the card game. I'm about to make contract."

♥ ♥ ♥

Helen was pouring coffee when the two men came in from their golf game. "So did either of you break par?"

"Waddya mean break par? We were both a couple strokes under." Gerald looked hurt.

"You must have used the ladies' tees." Sarah winked at Helen.

Jake put an arm on his new friend's shoulder. "Gerald here put me to shame. I barely broke par but he managed to get five birdies and only two bogies. Of course, he's familiar with the course. Give me a couple more times out there and I'll show him how it should be played."

The banter went back and forth for a half hour before Sarah suggested they get some of their things packed so they could hit the road early in the morning.

When back in Sarah's condo she felt strangely shy being alone with Jake. She found it hard to make eye contact, afraid of seeing love or need in his eyes. If he sensed her hesitation, he didn't say anything. By eight o'clock they had all but their bathroom essentials packed.

"Why don't we order something in for dinner? It'll save a

clean-up after."

"We could do that, Jake, or we could go around the corner for some meatballs and spaghetti."

"Let's go."

The easy banter between them put Sarah at ease and she realized that before long she was looking him in the eye again during their dinner conversation. She was grateful for having the kind of friends that help talk each other through difficult situations and never judge or question.

Chapter Twenty-seven

"Okay, do I have spaghetti sauce on my chin?" Jake patted around his mouth with his napkin.

"No. Why are you asking?"

"Because you keep looking at me like you want to say something."

"I ... I think. No, I know, that my friends think there is more between you and me than friendship."

"Ah. That's what has you uncomfortable. A blind man could see you weren't yourself when Gerald and I interrupted your bridge game."

"I'm that readable, am I?"

"Darlin', you might be an excellent bridge player but you're a lousy poker player. Your honest face shouts 'I don't like this hand I just got dealt'."

Sarah stabbed at a meatball then placed it back onto her plate. She reached across and laid her hand on Jake's. "That's where you're wrong, Jake. I've been dealt a nice hand ... a wonderful hand. I just don't know how to play it."

"Play it?" Jake took a large sip from his wine glass. "I'm not playing here, Sarah. Is that what you think? That I'm playing with you?"

"No, Jake. I was just following along with the card game

analogy you used." Sarah took her hand away and wiped her face with her own napkin. "Can we continue this upstairs?"

"Of course we can. I gotta find out what's bothering you. What I've done to make you so … subdued."

Jake paid the bill and followed Sarah in silence as they left the café and entered her building. On the elevator, she slid her arm through his and gave it a squeeze. "You're not going to the gallows, Jake. Don't look so solemn."

"You're scaring me, darlin'. I don't think I've seen you this serious before."

When they entered her condo unit, she offered to make decaf coffee but as she started to walk away, Jake took her and pulled her into an embrace. His searching eyes told her he wanted to get right to the conversation. She reached up and stroked his cheek.

"My friends have assumed that we are sleeping together. That we're a couple. That we're … that we love each other as more than just friends."

"And that appears to have really upset you." He released her from his embrace and ran a hand through his hair as if contemplating a difficult decision.

"It surprised more than upset me."

"Sarah, I —"

She interrupted him. "Let me finish." She took his hand and led him into the kitchen. "Sit." She pointed to a chair at the breakfast table then sat opposite him.

"How long have we been friends, Jake?"

His hand went to his hair again. "God, Sarah, I don't know. Seven, eight years anyway. Maybe longer. How long have we been wintering in the same building?"

"Exactly. We've been friends for so long we can't remember when or how it started. How *did* it start, Jake?"

"We just kept running into each other. Then, I don't know, maybe we had lunch or dinner together. Something like that."

"Something like that. Don't you see? Friends just seem to find each other and get comfortable — no strings attached. No first dates to remember. No anniversaries. Outside of remembering to call each other on birthdays friends are just … there." She was trying to read the expression in his eyes. Then saw that he appeared to be doing the same thing with her. She shifted her gaze to her own hands fidgeting with a piece of mail she'd left on the table.

"Helen started the conversation about us, you and me, today by commenting on how I always talked about what a nice guy you are but had never mentioned how sexy you are."

Jake jerked with surprised embarrassment. "Me? Sexy?"

"Her question surprised me because in that instant I realized I had always been looking at you through a friend's eyes, not a woman's eyes. I was so comfortable with our friendship that I forgot the relationship between you and me was not the same as between Helen, Olivia, Margaret, Stella and me. My female friends and I love each other. We hug. We kiss. We argue. We always, no matter what, support each other. Just like you and I do, Jake. That's why I was taken aback when Helen changed the context of our relationship — yours and mine. They all pointed out that you and I hug and kiss more than casual friends do."

She lifted her eyes to his again but couldn't read anything in them. He let his gaze drop to her fidgeting hand and placed his own on top of it.

"They even said we exchange more than friendly looks." This brought his eyes back to hers. "They suggested it's love for each other that we trade with our eyes. Romantic love, not friendly love."

He didn't say anything. He lifted her hand and wrapped it with his, not taking his eyes from hers.

Then finally, "And all these romantic suggestions have upset you."

Now it was her turn for silence.

She pulled her hand from his and stood by the window. When she turned, he was standing so close behind her she had to take a step back to look up at him.

"What I'm upset about, Jake, is that I wasn't upset. I was surprised more than upset. You've never pressed me for anything. We've had such a platonic relationship that I just never saw any signs. I never intended, nor even wanted, our friendship to become anything more. I guess Helen blindsided me with the fact that it has become more and I hadn't realized it."

She moved back to the table and slouched in the chair. Jake crouched down beside her. "Darlin' if you're no longer comfortable with me, with our friendship, relationship — whatever you want to call it …"

"Don't say it, Jake. Don't say anything. Hear me out. Please."

Chapter Twenty-eight

She looked at her watch and saw it was already past 8:00 p.m. They had told Gracie they would be in Montreal for a late breakfast, which meant leaving no later than 7:00 in the morning. This conversation was long overdue. She had never felt the need for it before but knew it had to be done to clear the air if not the tension.

"Let me make some decaf coffee. I have a long story to tell."

Sarah told Jake her whole story. How she had gotten pregnant and married young and the long-lasting consequences of that disastrous marriage. She explained how she had to work at two jobs after her husband, Tom Felstedt, deserted them, to keep her and their young daughter, Emily, housed and fed. One job was in the office of a large real estate office and the other was helping to cook, bake, serve and clean up when her boss's wife entertained wealthy clients in their home. All the while taking college courses to upgrade her office skills. This left her practically no time to spend with her toddler who spent most of her days with Sarah's mother and paid childcare, when necessary, until the child was old enough to be in school full days. When an opportunity for a full-time job in a government office came along, she took it. There she met a construction worker named

Gordon Hawkes. He was five years her senior and when she was twenty-eight and Emily ten years old, they got married. They had a son, Gordon Junior, and were extremely happy. Four years after their marriage, he was killed in an industrial accident. The company was found guilty of extreme workplace negligence and Sarah received a multi-million-dollar settlement. Gordon had a half-million-dollar insurance policy and another couple hundred thousand in investments. Sarah was financially able to stay home and care for three-year-old Junior and fourteen-year-old Emily. Her daughter was becoming more and more distant from Sarah resenting the fact that she had spent most of her childhood with her now-deceased grandparents and in daycare facilities while her brother was now getting all the care and attention from their mother that she had wished for and not received.

Sarah met her third husband, Harold Eisenboch, when she was thirty-four years old. It was Emily's second last year of high school and Junior was in kindergarten. They met when she became a member of the Ottawa Public Library Board where he had sat for several years. Harold was twenty years her senior and had lost his wife and young adult son in a car accident fifteen years earlier. He was a real estate agent and remembered Sarah from one of the parties she had catered years before. She later learned that he owned a number of rental properties. Their relationship started with casual coffees and then he invited her to a concert at the National Arts Centre. He met her children when he picked her up that evening and few weekends later, he invited them all for a day of skiing. The children liked him and he soon became a regular at their place for Sunday dinner and began taking Junior to hockey games. It was during this time that Emily and Sarah were able to spend more time together even though some coolness on Emily's part was ever present. Harold loved having children in his life again and while he was old enough to be their grandfather, being a part of a young family rejuvenated him and he attended all their events. He asked Sarah to marry him, she accepted and they were married just prior to her thirty-fifth birthday. They moved into a beautiful big home on the Ottawa River.

When Emily graduated from high school, she insisted on going to university in London, Ontario, where she met and married her husband, Daniel. They had two boys and eventually moved to Toronto.

"After seventeen years of a blissfully wonderful marriage, Harold died of natural causes. Emily was thirty-three years old. My two grandsons had called him Grandpa. He had always been in their lives. Junior was twenty-two, single and attending postgraduate school in New York studying finance. We were all devastated by Harold's death. He was such a kind, vibrant man. He filled our lives with his love and devotion. He left me an extremely wealthy woman and even left Emily's sons generous trust funds for their education.

"I was fifty-one, a multi-millionaire and so alone and heartbroken, I didn't know how I was going to survive without Harold in my life. I held on to all the rental properties and lived one day at a time. After five years I sold all the rental properties but two at sinfully high prices. I gave one each of the remaining properties to Junior and Emily. He was twenty-seven and she was thirty-seven by then. Junior moved back to Montreal and grew his inheritance considerably with the help of his degree in finance. He also advised me on investing my money. Emily wanted no advice from her brother choosing to go in her own direction. She rarely invites me to visit her and my grandsons. When she does, it's like a command performance at her convenience that I must attend whether the timing suits me or not.

"Junior married Sandra, an American as you know. They met while in college but the marriage didn't last. When she left him, she took Gracie and a considerable amount of money with her to New York. I was allowed very little contact with that grandchild. I built a survival net of sorts, I guess, and avoided children whenever I could. It broke my heart to be with other people's grandchildren and never able to enjoy my own. Instead, remembering my own early years, I use my money to financially help single mothers and neglected children.

"About a decade ago, I sold my home and bought this condo and my condo in Florida. I became friends with those three wonderful women I play bridge with and got on with my life. I have an amazing friend who owns a condo in the same building as mine in Florida. I've been quite content, summering here, wintering in Florida surrounded by the love of people close to me. Everyone accepts me for the person I am. No one knows how much money I have and no one cares. They know I'm comfortable but most of my donations are made anonymously so my name and wealth doesn't make the papers. I want for nothing except for the love of the two good men who provided me with the most wonderful years of my life.

"When Gordon was killed I thought my life had gone with him. It's my two children who kept me going. I never thought I could love a man again. But I did. Maybe I even loved Harold more. When he died, I wanted to jump in the ground with him. I didn't want to go on without him. I didn't think I could. I still miss him terribly. There isn't a day goes by that something doesn't remind me of him. Three husbands, Jake. I've had three husbands. How does the saying go? Two out of three ain't bad. I'm not blaming Tom for my first marriage. We were two young kids who thought we knew what love was. It wasn't until I met Gordon that I found out.

"I can't do four husbands, Jake. I just can't. When I told the girls that today they told me to not think about marriage — just enjoy being with someone I love. When I reminded them that two men I loved deeply had ended up dead, they smiled and told me that I should take good enough care of the next one to make sure he's the one who does the burying."

Jake had sat for over an hour listening to Sarah bare her soul to him. Now he silently slid an arm around her and just held her close. "Darlin', if I recall correctly, you're not yet sixty-five. Let's not talk about anybody getting buried for at least another thirty years. Most people retiring at our age have got big plans for a whole new life ahead of them."

He kissed her forehead. "I figure about twenty of those years we'll be healthy enough to keep travelling to Florida and being neighbours and friends. Whatever kind of friends we want to be."

When he received no response, he lifted her chin and looked into her eyes. "I love you, Sarah. No denying that and I'm guessing you've got some love in your heart for me too. Those last two husbands of yours seem like hard acts to follow, especially Harold. I'm not good at acting so I'll just tell you. I am who I am, Jakub Tatarek. An old retired guy from Chicago who wants you in my life any way I can have you. I spend my summers looking forward to the winters with you close by. Getting this chance to spend a couple weeks in the summer with you and your family is a real bonus. I'll go home and live on that until January. I'd like to spend twelve months a year with you but what I've got is better than not seeing you at all. Besides I kinda remember us talking about the possibility of a Hawaii trip in the fall. You going to renege on that?"

Sarah stared at Jake's moist eyes for several seconds. "I do have some love in my heart for you Jakub Tatarek from Chicago. It's the trip to Hawaii you promised me that's keeping me interested. In the meantime, we have another female who loves you and is waiting for you to take her fishing and the morning is going to come way too early."

She kissed him hard then messed his thick sandy-coloured hair laced abundantly with silver. "Your eyes lit up much too brightly when I said my friends think you're sexy looking."

Chapter Twenty-nine

"What time will we be getting up, Daddy?"

Gracie had her cell phone in her hands all ready to set the alarm on the clock, her excitement at going fishing in the morning all too evident in her face.

"Whenever we wake up." Gordon winked at Jake.

"What if we don't wake up until nine o'clock? The fish will have stopped biting by then. Jake said they usually feed first thing in the morning, around sunrise."

"Gracie, that will be before five o'clock in the morning. Surely you don't expect us to get up at four o'clock."

"Sunrise tomorrow will be 5:06 a.m."

Jake took pity on Gordon's dumbfounded look.

"Gracie, it's true. The fish feed best at sunrise but they still continue to nibble all morning long before they take their midday nap and then start biting again late in the afternoon. I was talking to our neighbour and he says the fishing has been pretty steady all morning long."

He wasn't sure if the look on Gracie's face was one of disappointment about not getting out on the lake at daybreak or disappointment at Jake's possible betrayal and dampening of her enthusiasm.

"How about we compromise a little?"

"Compromise how?" Gracie looked suspiciously at the two men.

"You set that alarm for 6:30. We'll get our gear all ready and waiting for us by the door and we'll be on the lake before 7:00."

"You promise?"

"I promise."

"I'll make breakfast sandwiches tonight and have the coffee pot set to start at 6:15 so you can eat and drink in the boat." Sarah felt sorry for the men who didn't appear to garner the respect of being the avid fishermen Gracie had placed on them.

"Aren't you coming with us, Grandma?"

"No. Jake doesn't need to oversee three novice fishermen in the boat on his first day of fishing. I'll wait till you guys get the hang of it then I'll join you. We have this cottage for five days so there's plenty of time. Besides I have to google how to cook walleyes so that I don't spoil our first fish feed."

One of his clients had learned of Gordon's search for a fishing cabin or resort where he could take his daughter, mother and a friend from Chicago for a few days. The man owned a cottage on a pretty good fishing lake within an hour's drive of Montreal and arranged for them to stay at a neighbour's cottage that would be empty for a couple of weeks. It came complete with a sixteen-foot fishing boat and motor. All they had to bring was linens, food and fishing gear. It even had satellite TV and Internet.

The three eager fishermen set about sorting their tackle and Jake saw about getting bait for the morning and making sure the gas tank on the boat was full. There were life jackets for all of them in the small boathouse by the water. A short while later, Sarah could hear the sound of a motor being started followed by Gracie's footsteps on the stairs.

"Grandma, come on. Jake wants to take a little ride to get the feel of the boat and check out the shoreline."

"Okay, sweetie. I'll be right there."

Gracie ran back down to the dock with Sarah not far behind.

Sarah had to admit the boat ride was a relaxing and enjoyable experience. Jake certainly knew how to handle the boat and seemed to be enjoying the opportunity to be out on the water and explaining how to steer the boat to Gracie. It wasn't long before he let her take over the wheel while he squatted behind her and handled the speed controls.

❦ ❦ ❦

The next morning, the fish that Jake promised would be biting, soon were taking the bait and they were even putting some back, choosing only the right size and amount for a fish fry for supper. Gracie was heartbroken she couldn't keep them all, but Jake explained the responsibility of taking only what was necessary. They were back at the cabin by lunch time with a stringer of nice eating-size fish and a beaming Gracie wanting pictures taken of their catch. She watched as Jake filleted them and prepared them for the fridge in anticipation of their supper later.

The warm June temperatures held with only one cloudy day during their time at the lake. Sarah managed to land a few fish herself, making sure pictures of her were taken as well. Jake and Gordon bonded like a father and son. Sarah watched the older man in his element teaching the younger man and the eager teenager how to start the motor and drive the boat. He showed Gordon how to maintain control of the vessel while landing a fish. Under his direction they learned the difference between still-fishing, drifting and trolling; what types of lures were used for each and how much line to let out for each. They learned how to find the bottom and then lift their lines just enough to find where the hungry fish were feeding. Most importantly, he taught them how to unsnag their lines without losing their lures or bait.

❦ ❦ ❦

They stayed a few more days in Montreal visiting the tourist sites and touring Old Montreal. Sarah never got tired of visiting the old historical buildings and sampling the cuisine and fine dining in that part of the city. Gracie appeared to be as enthralled with the waterfront and food as much as anything New York had to offer. The fact that the signs and conversations were predominantly in French was a novelty to her.

❣ ❣ ❣

The evening before Sarah and Jake were to return to Ottawa, Gracie knocked on Sarah's bedroom door. "Can I come in?"

"Certainly, darling. Come sit and chat with me. I'm just getting my things ready for my trip back."

"Did you enjoy our fishing trip, Grandma?"

"I sure did. I can't remember having so much fun in a long time."

"I did too." She picked up a pair of her grandmother's earrings and held them up to her own ears, admiring them in the mirror. "Will you and Jake be able to come back again this summer?"

Sarah smiled. "I'm glad you and Jake got to have a fun fishing trip together. I think he enjoyed it as much as you did." She placed a couple more items inside her suitcase. "I think you're forgetting that Jake doesn't live in Ottawa. Chicago is much farther and not a convenient drive away."

"I know, but he's retired and he doesn't have any family in Chicago. Maybe he could move to Ottawa and then he'd be close to all of us. We're almost like family."

Sarah noticed tears in Gracie's eyes an instant before the young girl buried herself in her grandmother's embrace.

Chapter Thirty

"Wanna talk about it?" Helen had invited Sarah to come for lunch while the two men were at the golf course.

"What do you mean? Talk about what?"

"Sarah, you've been back home for three days. Jake can't stop talking about the good time he had, how great the fishing was, how well Gordon and Gracie had caught on to the fine art of fishing and you have not said a word."

When Sarah didn't respond, Helen repeated, "Do you want to talk about it or not? If not, I won't ask again but I can see something is bothering you."

Sarah nodded at her friend. "Yes, something happened. Is happening. I just don't know if it's a good thing or a bad thing."

"Whatever it is doesn't seem to be affecting Jake so it must be something between you and Gordon or Gracie. Or maybe something involving Jake that he's not aware of?"

"It's the latter."

"Jake?"

"Yes." Sarah toyed with the remains of a pasta salad on her plate. "This is delicious by the way. You added something that I don't recognize."

"I just used a store-bought dressing rather than my own."

"It's good."

"Sarah?"

Helen stood and removed their plates. Poured more coffee

into Sarah's half-empty cup and placed a platter of tarts on the table.

"Gracie slept in my bed with me the last night we were there."

"Was she not feeling well?"

"She was feeling some pending lonesomeness I think. She really enjoyed her time with Jake and me. More so Jake than me I suspect but he is the fishing expert after all." She glanced out the window then placed a tart on her napkin. "That poor child is in a strange city with no one but her father. It's not just a new city; it's truly a strange city to her."

"In what way?"

"She enjoyed the novelty of listening to people speak a different language at first. She had fun reading the signs and trying to translate them. Gordon had hoped to keep her busy by enrolling her for a track meet but most of the participants were all previous friends who mostly spoke French. She told me she realized then just how different her old home and her new home are. She said she tried to accept that it's no different than moving to a European country and having to learn a new language but she's also trying to get used to life without her mother at a time when she really needs her. I know Gordon is trying to do everything he can to ease her into this new life, but I think he's worried she may decide she wants to go back."

"The poor kid has been through so much. I can't imagine what it must be like for her." Helen placed her hand on Sarah's. "What do you think? Do you have the same fear?"

Sarah took a bite from the sweet butter tart.

"I am afraid of that, yes. Maybe her other grandparents were right. Maybe she does belong in New York."

"Nonsense. Thousands, hundreds of thousands, of children have made new homes in strange countries and survived. It's just getting over the initial loneliness. She did have an overprotective mother who wouldn't let her have any thoughts of her own. I think it will just take time for her to realize she can think for herself, make decisions for herself and choose her own friends."

"She asked me if Jake and I can come back again over the summer."

"Well, you certainly don't have anything stopping you but that's a long way for Jake to make a second trip in quick succession."

"I told her that."

"I'm sure she understands."

"She thinks Jake should move here. She feels he has absolutely nothing holding him in Chicago and he has a loving *almost* family here in Canada."

"Oh my."

"Exactly."

"What does Jake think about that?"

"He doesn't know she asked me about it."

"She didn't suggest it to him then?"

"I begged her not to. I had to." Her voice tightened and she stood.

"Helen, I can't ask Jake to uproot himself, give up his home and move to a different country on the whim of a lonesome child! Make that teenager. I was reminded steadily that since her birthday she's not a child anymore. Anyway, I'm not ready for him to take up residence here even if he wanted to. She's expecting me to broach the idea to him. The promise of me doing that was the only way I could keep her from asking him herself.

"I honestly don't know what to do. She truly loves him. She even asked me if I thought he would let her call him Grandpa since he seems like a grandpa to her. And I think he loves her too. I think he loves her enough that he would feel extreme guilt at letting her down if he wasn't of a mind to make such an extreme change in his life. I ... I don't think I want to lay that on him."

"Do you think he would even consider it?"

"I don't know. Us being together a good part of the year is far different from one of us giving up our home for the other. That's a … a real commitment. I can't speak for him but I'm not sure I'm ready for him to be that big a part of my life. I like my life the way it is."

She paced the dining room floor finally placing her hands on the back of the chair she had been sitting in. "I knew things would get out of hand if I let my guard down. Why is this happening?"

"Why is what happening, darlin'? Is something wrong?"

Neither of the women had heard the men come in the door and down the hall.

Chapter Thirty-one

Helen's quick thinking saved the moment for Sarah.

"We were just talking about the responsibilities Sarah is being asked to take on for the fundraising. It seems her Winter Gala was such a success they want to slide a couple of new projects by her for her to consider taking over."

Sarah mouthed a thank you to her friend.

"Well, girl, I hope these new projects won't keep you from going to Hawaii with me. I'm hoping we can nail down some dates and reservations before I leave."

"Hawaii, yes. We'll have to make some definite plans for sure. I won't let anything interfere with that."

❣ ❣ ❣

They decided to cross the river into Quebec for supper. She had not yet taken him to the Champlain Lookout situated in the Gatineau Hills from where a good part of the Ottawa Valley could be seen.

"You have to see this view in late September — if you can get near it. The view is spectacular. The colours are indescribable. I never tire of it. The only downside, or upside, I guess that depends on those who benefit, is that tourists flock in by the thousands. If you think the traffic jam in Chicago is bad during rush hour, you don't want to try navigating these hills at the height of autumn colours season."

"It's hard to believe it can get much better than this but I guess a view in technicolour must be something to see." He wrapped an arm around her shoulders. "You sure do live in a beautiful part of the world. I guess us Americans should sometimes think north instead of south when we make our travel plans. We don't appreciate our beautiful neighbour enough."

Sarah laughed. "I think you Yanks see Canada as a land of igloos and vast expanses of snow, so cold that all our birds have to fly south to escape the temperatures. Human as well as feathered. We are fortunate enough to celebrate all four seasons up here, each having its own distinct pleasures."

"Guilty on almost all counts. Chicago sits on one of the Great Lakes so I know what winter and snow are all about. However, I never realized that mountains and scenery like this existed east of the Rocky Mountains in Canada. Or that your summers can get so hot." He ran a hand through his hair. "I hope I haven't worn out my welcome, Sarah, because I'd like to come and experience all four of those seasons. You're a good tourism promoter."

"Well, I hear the fishing is good in September so you might want to pencil in a trip up here on your calendar. I know a certain young lady who would be delighted to see you again."

"And I know a lady of a certain age that I hope might welcome me back also."

"Of course." Sarah slid her arm through his and steered him toward her car. "You might think about planning it to include our Thanksgiving."

♥ ♥ ♥

"So let me get this straight. You are not interested in getting married a fourth time. You love your independence and freedom to come and go as you please. A man to tie you down is the last thing that you want. Jake is a super nice man but just a friend. A good friend."

"A good friend with benefits." Helen interrupted Olivia.

"Helen!" Sarah frowned at her.

"Oh, come on, Sarah." Olivia laid her cards face down on the dining room table. "We're just having a problem with your reasoning. You say you're not interested in a relationship but you seem to enjoy him immensely when he's around. We're having a problem accepting your denials of feelings for Jake when he's becoming more and more a big part of your life and that of your family as well."

"Well, Helen, one item that can be put to rest is that I am not sleeping with him. What's more, it's no one's business if I were. But I'm not." Sarah placed her cards on the table as well. "Jake really is a super nice man and a good friend. We enjoy each other's company immensely. He knows I am not interested in a more permanent relationship and he's good with that. I'm good friends with all of you and have enjoyed sharing vacations with a couple of you. I treasure our time together also so why is it different because Jake is a man?"

Margaret took Sarah's hand and squeezed it. "There's a difference between loving a friend and being in love with a friend."

"I'm not in love with him."

"A blind person could see that he's in love with you, Sarah." Margaret smiled at her friend. "It's time to stop denying your feelings for him as well."

Sarah pulled her hand free and sat back in her chair. Three pairs of eyes were staring at her waiting for a response.

"I'm not in love with him. I … I …" She looked at each set of eyes and felt the moisture build in her own. "Dear God, I … I can't be in love with him."

"Why not?" Olivia saw a tear slip from Sarah's eye.

"Because I care about him too much to let myself fall in love with him. I should have nipped this in the bud. I shouldn't have allowed it to have gone this far."

"Well, now I think we're even more confused." Margaret spoke softly.

"I'll ask you again. Why can't you allow yourself to fall in love with Jake?"

"You know why, Olivia."

"Jake isn't going to die, Sarah."

"What?" Margaret and Helen asked in unison.

"Sarah is not allowing herself to get too close to another man because she has buried two men who loved her. It's fear that's keeping her from opening her heart to Jake. She's afraid he'll die too."

"That is ridiculous." Helen walked around the table to give her friend's shoulder a squeeze.

"No. It's not." Sarah blotted her eyes with a tissue. "Jake is not a young man. He's overweight. He eats the wrong food. Golfing is the only exercise he gets. He's a prime candidate for a heart attack. He … he … Oh, God. Why did I have to meet him in the first place."

Helen hugged her. "When Edward walked out on me I felt it was my fault he had looked elsewhere. I thought I must be lacking in what keeps a man interested. I must be too boring. Too ugly. Too fat. Too skinny. Too … everything that would turn my husband away from me. I hated myself more than I hated him and believe me, hate is too mild a word for what I felt for him. When I met Gerald, I was afraid he would lose interest just like Edward did. Especially when Stella, bless her heart, started baking for him and seemed to be there for him when I was so self-absorbed in getting my business up and running. I told myself it would only be a matter of time until he got bored with me anyway. I wasn't going to let that happen again." She took a deep breath. "Is that what you're afraid of, Sarah? Afraid of the pain of having your heart wrenched right out of you again? Because if it is, then you may be letting your fear deprive you of some of the best years of your life. Jake knows two men you loved have died and he's not afraid. Just as Gerald wasn't afraid to take a chance on a poor, pathetic loser like me. I thank my lucky stars every day that he did."

Sarah looked at each of her friends. "I know it's hard for you to understand but I'm quite happy the way things are. Jake and I have been close friends every winter for the past few years and now we'll probably be seeing each other a little more often. I have Gracie to thank for that. But I'm still not keen on letting it become anything more than what it is."

"You're trying to trick fate by pretending not to care as much as you do. Fate has nothing to do with it my friend. God does. And none of us knows what He has in store. Maybe Jake will be the one left to mourn. And if that happens, he will thank God for giving him a number of wonderful years with you." Margaret sat back down. "Now, let's get this card game finished so we can have some of whatever smells so delightful in the kitchen."

Chapter Thirty-two

The end of June usually meant a slowdown with a number of Sarah's board meetings. Everyone seemed to need a summer break. The only fundraiser with which she was involved over the summer was a half marathon that contributed major funding for one of the hospital foundations. The soup kitchen was grateful for an extra day of her help over the summer when many of their regular volunteers went to their various cottages for the summer. It was while serving a meal at one of the downtown locations that she noticed a man who looked very much like her homeless man walk out of the washroom, nod at the coordinator and stride out the front door. He stopped to chat with a man on the street for a moment before disappearing out of sight. He was clean and neatly dressed so she thought perhaps she was mistaken, although he did walk with a slight limp.

Later when they were wiping down the kitchen and mopping the floor, the coordinator came out of his office and approached Sarah to thank her for coming in an extra day to help with the meals. She smiled graciously and commented on the hard work of all the kitchen staff who didn't seem to mind working in an overheated kitchen. He was walking toward his office again when she remembered the man she had seen a little earlier.

She called his name. "Joe, can I ask you who the man was that I saw come from the washroom and nod at you an hour or so ago?"

Joe hesitated for a second and she thought maybe he was trying to remember the incident but then he reminded her that they don't discuss individuals who come and go from the soup kitchens.

Sarah knew this and should have known better than to ask. She wouldn't like her name given out to anyone.

"I'm sorry. I do know that. He just reminded me of someone I've been trying to locate."

"You know that most of the people who come here don't want to be located. Most are trying to isolate themselves from anyone looking for them." He smiled at Sarah. "I wish I could help you, Sarah. I know you mean no harm to anyone."

"That's okay. I understand." She turned her attention back to the floor she was mopping then looked up once again. "I just wish there was some way I could communicate with him."

"If it helps at all, I can tell you that I don't know the man's name. He goes by several aliases that change by the month it seems. None of which I can give you anyway."

"If he's the man I've been looking for, he certainly was a lot cleaner today than the last time I saw him."

"That happens." Joe turned quickly and shut himself inside his office.

Sarah finished her cleaning and decided to take a quick walk through the market. She hadn't gone quite a block toward it when she spotted the man who had been standing outside the soup kitchen and with whom her homeless man had stopped to chat. She didn't hesitate in walking right up to him.

"I'm hoping you can help me. I noticed that you were outside the soup kitchen earlier and that a man who had been inside stopped to chat with you. I've been trying to chat with that man and can never seem to catch up to him. Can you tell me where I might find him?"

"I don't remember talking to anybody, lady. I think you got

me mixed up with somebody else."

He was moving away and about to turn his back on her.

"Look, I understand if you don't want to tell me where he is or what his name is. My name is Sarah and I work at the soup kitchen every Wednesday. If you see him, can you tell him I'd like to talk with him please? I owe him an apology."

"I know where you work. I see you there all the time." He turned then and hurried away.

♥♥♥

Gordon brought Gracie to Ottawa the next week and left her to stay with Sarah for a week while he went on to a finance seminar in Toronto. Sarah took the opportunity to take Gracie on tours of several of the museums in Ottawa and Gatineau. The girl soaked up all the Canadian history that she could. She was mesmerized by the exhibitions at the National Art Gallery as well. Sarah was relieved and delighted that Gracie showed so much interest in her father's country. Actually, it was her country also since she had been born in Montreal before her mother had left the marriage and the country, taking the child with her. The thought of Gracie wanting to return to the United States was a constant niggle at the back of Sarah's mind. The more she could help her feel a kinship to Canada, the more it would lessen the odds of her feeling that the USA was home.

Of course a day at a spa in Wakefield was a must-do. Helen was happy to join them and Margaret's step-granddaughter, Kelly, came along also. The two girls were only a couple of years apart so each was quite pleased to have someone in their own age group for company.

"Daddy, I'd really like to stay a little longer if Grandma will let me." Gordon had called from Toronto to let his daughter know that he'd be picking her up the next day.

"So you're having fun?"

"Yes! We've been going out to museums every day and I'm

learning so much about Canada. Today we went to a spa and I made a new friend. She's a granddaughter of one of Grandma's friends and she lives right here in this building. We would like to have a sleepover before I go back home. Kelly, that's my friend's name, wants to take me to the Museum of Science one day next week and there's a new movie we both want to see." She stopped only long enough to catch her breath then continued. "Daddy, I can't go home yet. I just can't. Please?"

"It certainly sounds like you're having a great time, sweetie. Maybe I should talk to your grandmother."

Sarah took the phone and confirmed that all was good. She was happy that Gracie had found a friend her age in the building and that everything was agreed upon among all the grandparents concerned. Gordon confirmed she could stay one more week but then she must return to Montreal for a full schedule of sports activities coming up.

❦ ❦ ❦

The following week, Sarah dropped the girls off at the movie theatre before she went to the soup kitchen to help serve that day's meal. Margaret was to pick the girls up when the movie was finished.

"Kelly, make sure you call your grandmother as soon as the movie is finished. I may have to stay a little longer to help prep some food for tomorrow's meal. I think Margaret is planning a nice supper for the two of you." She winked at them as she moved away. She knew that Margaret and Clarke were planning on taking the girls for a quick bite, then on a Rideau Canal cruise.

❦ ❦ ❦

She was about to exchange her apron for a broom after the meal was served when she sensed someone staring at her. Looking up, she was startled to see her street person standing inside the entrance watching her. Afraid if she spoke she might spark another hasty retreat on his part, she stood her ground and stared right back in silence. He appeared to be taking in her appearance from head to toe. She did the same to him. He was clean, wearing denim cut-offs and sandals. The man didn't look threatening at all. In fact, he seemed wary and unsure of himself. He was leaning against the door frame with arms crossed casually but one finger was strumming against the elbow it was clasping.

"Can I help you?" Sarah stood still as she asked the question.

"Are you Sarah?"

"Yes, I am."

"I was informed you want to talk to me. That you owe me an apology if I understand correctly."

His speech was clear. No hesitation and well-enunciated.

"I believe we've met before."

Now she did sense hesitation … and something else. Not fear. Not disdain. More like caution. His dark eyes reminded her of the cold night she had looked into them before. Who was this man?

Chapter Thirty-three

Margaret reached Sarah's voicemail for the second time. She had wanted to let Sarah know that the girls had been picked up, fed and were waiting in line to board the cruise boat in the canal. She had tried Sarah's landline at home only to receive a similar voicemail message.

"Your grandma must be getting her hair done or met someone for dinner. She's not picking up her phone." She spoke to Gracie who had tried to reach her grandmother as well.

"She didn't say she was meeting anyone but she might have run into someone she knows." Gracie didn't seem concerned. "Grandma knows so many people. Every time we go anywhere, we have to keep stopping to talk to someone she knows. She doesn't like it when I answer my phone when we're eating or doing something together so I guess that's why she's not picking up."

"I'm sure she'll be home before us and if not, then you can wait for her at our place." Clarke ushered them all aboard and then relying on a cane for support, he followed them on to the boat.

♥ ♥ ♥

When the man hadn't responded, Sarah removed her apron and threw it into a bin for the soiled kitchen linens. She looked at him again as she reached for a broom and moved around to the front of the serving table. He hadn't budged. Nor had he taken his eyes from her. She could hear a couple other volunteers talking out of view in the kitchen where they were preparing vegetables for the next day's meal. The knowledge of others within hearing distance helped her maintain confidence in her own safety, although the man didn't have a threatening appearance. He seemed calm and watchful, waiting for her to continue the conversation.

She started sweeping the floor and noticed him picking up chairs and placing them upside down on the tables. He wasn't going anywhere but neither was he talking.

"You visited the building I live in last winter." She glanced over at him to see his reaction.

There was none.

"It was a very cold night and I believe you were seeking shelter from it in our entryway."

He was nonresponsive. Was he playing a game? His back was to her as he continued to lift chairs for her to sweep under. She could see a fair amount of grey mixed in with his dark hair. The mix and texture, even the shape of his head seemed slightly familiar. Had she met him before without realizing it? She tried to think where it might have been. Where had she been since last January that she unknowingly might have run into him?

He turned and caught her staring at him.

His mouth finally opened. "Go on."

Startled, she was slow to respond. "It appears you have received some assistance."

"What makes you say that?"

She didn't know how to respond without insulting him. How could she say he looked cleaner, smelled better, than he had then? That he didn't look like the smelly heap of old blankets and dirty clothes that he had then? That he had seemed deserving of the toe of her boot back then?

He had stopped mid-lift of a chair and was studying her. His eyes moving back and forth looking deeply into both of hers. She put a hand on the chair he was holding and moved it back to the floor.

"Who are you?"

"You didn't ask me that that night." His voice was steady. Not accusing. Not angry.

"That's why I owe you an apology." She breathed a sigh of relief. Relief at finally having an opportunity to try to make things right with this homeless man who could easily have frozen to death so many months ago because of her unkindness.

She slumped into the chair he had just set back on the floor. Her shoulders shook as she started to cry. He didn't comfort her. He didn't reach for her. He merely pulled another chair near and sat down across from her.

"I tried to find you after. I searched the streets for you for several nights. I even checked out the men's shelters trying to find you."

"Why?"

"Because I was haunted by you. Haunted by my own guilt and shame. When I poked you with my boot to see if you were alive and you looked at me through the opening in your blanket, I felt absolute shame at having kicked you. I was so stunned that a human being was actually alive inside that bundle on the freezing sidewalk, I was momentarily immobilized. By the time I realized what I had done, what had just happened, you were already hurrying out of earshot and didn't hear me holler after you. You disappeared so quickly I couldn't find you.

"I was so afraid you were going to die in that cold that I couldn't sleep. A friend came home moments later and invited me in to her place to talk about it. I kept watching out my window for you to return but you never did.

"I'm certain I've seen you around the Byward Market several times but you always disappeared before I could call out to you.

It was as if you were purposely avoiding me."

She stood and reached for a paper napkin to wipe her damp cheeks and nose. A couple weeks ago I saw you come out of the washroom and nod at Joe then stop and talk to someone on the street outside. I asked Joe who you were but of course he can't disclose names of any of the patrons or volunteers here. I did find the man you spoke to on the street and asked him to relay my message to you."

"Why was it so important to you?"

"I had to know that you were all right. All winter I had visions of you freezing to death on the street. I felt that I would have been responsible because I didn't help you that night. I … I … just wanted to tell you how sorry I was for being so cruel. I just wanted to try to make it up to you somehow. I … just had to beg for your forgiveness. Which I don't really deserve."

The man stood and walked toward the door. He put his hand on the bar to open it then turned. He opened his mouth as if to speak. Sarah watched as he seemed to be thinking about something, maybe what he should say or do … Then he turned and stepped out the door. As it swung shut, Sarah could hear his voice saying, "I forgive you."

Chapter Thirty-four

Sarah walked over to the Notre Dame Basilica. She wasn't Catholic but she knew it was a stop she had to make. Gracie and the Ingrams would be wondering where in the world she was but she couldn't go straight home. She would call them as soon as she finished this errand.

Evening Mass was just concluding when she entered. She slid into a pew near the rear of the beautiful church. She knelt and bowed her head. "Thank you."

❣ ❣ ❣

She had called Gracie as soon as she was back on the street and apologized for being AWOL for a couple of hours. Her explanation was that someone she knew had come in to the soup kitchen and had needed her attention. When pressed for details, Sarah evaded any further discussion by deceptively deploying Joe's excuse of not being able to discuss the private goings-on at that location. Olivia raised an eyebrow at the feeble excuse when they next played cards, but the others seemed to accept it.

Gracie had gone home to Montreal at the end of her second week and appeared to have settled into her sports activities quite well. Her earlier unease at being in a different country with a different culture seemed to have ebbed. Sarah hoped that learning some of the Canadian history and way of life from visiting the local museums might have helped. She at least had a better understanding and respect for the reasoning behind the two national languages.

Sarah felt somewhat unsettled after her encounter with the homeless man at the shelter. Outside of his forgiveness she was no further ahead in identifying him or what had become of him over the balance of the winter and spring. By his clean appearance she surmised that he may have found employment even though he still seemed to inhabit the area around the shelter. He had not returned to the soup kitchen in the following two weeks. She still didn't know his name or what had caused his homelessness in the first place. Did he have a family? Was he from around Ottawa? Was he a criminal? Have an addiction? Was there some way she could help him?

♥♥♥

"You've not been yourself these last few weeks. Is something bothering you?" Olivia was sharing a late afternoon cup of tea with Sarah.

"I'm fine. Maybe just a little at loose ends with not as much to do these days."

"I think it's more than that."

Sarah took another bite of her lemon tart. She swallowed it and washed it down with a sip of tepid tea.

"I finally met the homeless man from last winter."

Olivia almost choked on her tea.

"You what?"

"I met the man I kicked on our doorstep in January."

"When? Where? Why have you not said anything?"

"I can't talk about it because it involves the shelter where I help with meals."

"What do you mean you can't talk about it? He has been haunting you for half a year and you can't talk about it?"

"The clients there are protected by privacy rules."

"I see." Olivia played with her spoon. "Can you at least say whether you made peace with him? With yourself?"

"Outside of having received his forgiveness, I can't say that I am any clearer on who he is or why he was on the street in the freezing cold. So yes, I have made peace with him but no, I have not made peace with myself."

"How did you meet him?"

"I can't say."

"Will you see him again?"

"That I don't know. If I do, it will be by accident."

"How was he? Does he seem like a nice person?"

"Yes. He does."

"Does he appear to be healthy?"

"Yes. He does."

"Then you've met him. You've probably explained yourself to him. He's forgiven you. You've seen that he's alive and well and probably moving on with his life so why are you so upset? Isn't that exactly what you wanted to happen?"

"I thought it was but now I wish I knew more about him. I have so many questions that still remain unanswered."

"Maybe you'll run into him again and he'll open up more."

"Maybe. There's just something about him. Something I can't explain. It's like I've opened a door and something on the other side is calling me to walk through. I need to know what's on the other side."

"Sarah Eisenboch, you are always looking for more. More what? None of us knows. You can never settle, can you? Anyone else would be happy to have met the man they felt they had abused and received his forgiveness, but not you. You need to know every little why, what, when and where. If the man wants you to know more, he knows where to find you. If he doesn't, then be grateful for this much and move on. Have you forgotten that you have a trip to Hawaii to plan and a Thanksgiving dinner with house guests to look forward to? And possibly another Quebec fishing trip before the summer is over? You have too much on your plate to be dwelling on the past. The man obviously doesn't want you to know anything more about him. Accept that."

Sarah nodded and carried her plate and cup to the sink. "You're right. In fact I have a message from Jake to call him. I better go back upstairs and do just that."

She stopped in the hallway to give Olivia a hug. "You are so wise. I wish I was more like you sometimes. Thank you for being a good friend and keeping me on the right track. When you tell the girls about my encounter with the homeless man … Don't shake your head. I know you will. You can tell them that I'm taking your advice and being grateful for at least having found him."

❣ ❣ ❣

"Jake, I'm glad you called. We have to discuss our trip to Hawaii. I have some ideas about it."

"Do you, darlin'? I keep waiting for you to tell me you've changed your mind about going."

"Why would I do that?"

"You have such a busy life, I'm afraid something is going to come up that will bump our trip to a back burner."

"On the contrary, I've bowed out of two of my fund raisers that I usually chair. I told them I'm getting too old and they had best look for younger blood and younger ideas."

"You know they'll be calling you to pick your brain and looking for any help you can give them. You've been at this too long for your experience to go to waste."

"You may be right, but I've decided it's time for me to enjoy some downtime. Besides there's this old guy I know who's been after me to do some travelling with him. I better get on board before he changes his mind."

"No chance of that, Sarah. Now what are these ideas of yours about Hawaii?"

She explained that with all the traveling he'd be doing going back and forth between Chicago, Ottawa and Montreal and back again then on to Hawaii that maybe he should think about combining some of it. They discussed all the possibilities and decided that the fishing trip in Quebec be delayed by a week or so to facilitate his stay for Thanksgiving. She would accompany him back to Chicago after Thanksgiving and they would fly from there to Hawaii.

"Do you think you can put up with me for all that time?"

"Jake, it's only about six weeks. We spend way more than that together when we're in Florida."

"Not under the same roof, darlin'. We have our separate homes there."

"Are you worried? Do you want to rent separate accommodations in Hawaii?"

"Not at all. I'm worried because I know you like your space."

"Jake, I'm learning that your being in my space isn't necessarily a bad thing." There she had said it. Let the pieces fall where they may.

There was silence on the other end of the line. Maybe Jake liked having his space too and had just never mentioned it. Maybe he was having doubts about all that togetherness also. Maybe she and her friends had read him wrong.

"Jake?"

"I'm here, darlin'. I was just waiting to see if you were being serious or maybe a delayed laugh was coming."

"Jake, we get along really well. If we can enjoy being together for a few weeks, I don't see why it can't work for six or so weeks."

"I agree. I think it's a great idea. It sure saves on a lot of back and forth air fare and driving. I've been hoping you might want to see my place and a little bit of Chicago at some point anyway.

Ya see? Even at your age you still have great ideas."

She could hear the humour in his statement.

"Okay, we just have to tell Miss Gracie that her fishing trip is going to be delayed by a week or so. Maybe it will go down easier if it comes from you."

Jake laughed. "All right, darlin', I'll be the bad guy."

"You know you could never be the bad guy in her eyes, Jake. She loves you."

Chapter Thirty-five

Sarah took to wandering the market. She found shops, restaurants and boutiques she didn't know had existed. All the while she was aware of everyone she passed on the streets. Often, she faked phone conversations so that she could sit and look around while pretending to be talking on the phone. All the shady places to relax with a cold drink became familiar rest stops for her. She recognized the faces that passed by at the same times every day. Once a man offered to buy her an iced coffee and to join her at her table. She had to do some fast talking to discourage him politely. Vendors who rented tables by the day came and went with their wares. Some interested her, others were merely repeats of the same type of merchandise just different designs or colours. Several times her heart skipped a beat when she thought her homeless person was nearby but after a couple of weeks of watching and waiting, she realized that wasn't going to happen. He had disappeared. But to where?

♥ ♥ ♥

Gordon told her he was thinking of taking Gracie to New York for a week or so to visit her maternal grandparents. The apartment that was owned by him and Gracie was going to be vacant in the latter part of July and early August.

"It's a good opportunity for us to spend some time there and Gracie has been asking to see them."

"I guess it's better than sending her to stay with them. She'll probably feel more at ease in the home she's familiar with."

"I'm wondering about that. I hope it doesn't spark some sad feelings that might lead to worse feelings."

"Have you got someone you can ask about that? Your family doctor maybe?"

"I talked to her track coach whom she seems to have bonded with and she feels Gracie's strong enough to deal with it. Madeline's going to have a talk with her after their meet this evening."

"Madeline?"

"Gracie's coach."

"That's a great idea, Gordie. She would be objective in her opinion. Let me know what she thinks."

"I will, Mom. Jake called the other day and told Gracie he's going to have to delay his fishing trip up here for a week or two. If I take Gracie to New York for a visit, it might shorten the wait for her to get fishing again. Jake also told her that he hopes she's been practising her piano because he wants to hear her play when he comes up again. If she's mastered a new song by then, he'll take her white-water rafting in Ottawa while he's up this way. It's given her something else to focus on."

"Trust Jake to come up with something like that to soften the blow of a fishing delay."

Thank you, Jake.

♥ ♥ ♥

"Jake's gonna go white-water rafting? Is he nuts?" Margaret looked aghast when Sarah told them about Jake's ploy to get Gracie working on her piano skills.

"I think that's admirable of him." Stella, who was filling in for Olivia for bridge, smiled as she shuffled the cards.

"I don't know if admirable is the right word but it's certainly big of him to put the offer out there." Helen picked up her cards and sorted them.

"I admire a man who would go to such lengths for a child he obviously cares for. He seems to want her to hone her artistic skills as well as her athletic and outdoors interests. Not many men would give a hoot about whether a child plays the piano or not. Good for Jake."

"I never thought of it that way, Stella, but you're absolutely right. The man should be commended for wanting Gracie to have a well-rounded outlook." Margaret hesitated before starting the bidding. "I was thinking more of his physical limitations. At our ages we have to be careful what we choose to participate in and I would think that paddling through white water in a rubber raft might be pretty demanding."

Sarah laughed. "Don't tell Jake he might not be able to do something. He'll double his efforts to prove you wrong. I worry about his heart but he's got stamina I never believed him capable of."

Helen smirked. "Stamina in a man is important."

"Really, Helen. I don't know where your mind takes you sometimes. I was referring to the hiking in the mountains that he did on our return trip from Florida last winter. I was exhausted but he took those trails like nobody's business. Maybe it's from walking the golf courses but the man is stronger than he looks."

"Talking about all that walking in the mountains, Jake has asked Clarke and me about some of the sightseeing we did during our trip to Hawaii last spring. I guess he's getting serious about your Hawaii vacation plans and is looking at different tours and which islands to explore. Have you set a date for that, Sarah?"

"Not a definite date. We're talking about sometime shortly after Thanksgiving."

"Will you fly from here?"

"No. We've decided it might be best if I go down to Chicago with him when he leaves and we'll fly from there to Hawaii."

All eyes shifted from cards to Sarah's face.

"You're going to Chicago? You're going to Jake's place?" Helen voiced the question for everyone.

"Yes."

Margaret leaned forward. "I know that's the economical thing to do but is it the smart thing to do?"

"Look, I know what you're thinking. That I'm maybe leading Jake on. Giving him expectations that maybe I shouldn't be, but my gut is telling me this is the way to go." Sarah looked at each of her friends. "I don't know if I'm being smart or foolish but it seems right."

Stella looked at Sarah. "I'm not sure of all the dynamics at play here and maybe it's not my place to comment but from a woman who has missed so many opportunities for happiness, I think if something feels right, then do it. Jake seems like a kind, caring man and if your decision is bringing you both some happiness then don't let the opportunity slip by." She placed a hand on Sarah's. "Believe me when I tell you that loneliness is always accompanied by a feeling of 'if only'. I envy that life has given you some wonderful opportunities and I applaud you for having taken them. If you hadn't, you might be sitting alone in your apartment thinking 'if only I had.' You are a good person. Jake seems like a good person. If you can make each other happy, then do so. Enjoy each moment together." Her voice broke and she stopped. "Oh dear, look at who is giving who advice here. Look at where my choices have brought me. I must learn to keep my thoughts to myself. Forgive me."

Sarah placed her other hand on top of Stella's. "Nothing to forgive. I thank you for your wise words. Sometimes, a person sitting on the edge can see things better than someone caught up in the middle. I will take your advice to heart and remember it when I doubt whether my choice regarding Jake seems right or not. I'll remember to think about whether it will bring happiness or not. Thank you."

She withdrew her hands and looked around the table. "Yes. I am going to Chicago. I am visiting Jake on his turf. I felt his happiness through the phone when I told him so. You have all been right. I've been fortunate to have had two men in my life, both of whom brought so much happiness into it. Maybe it's time for me to give some away — to a man well deserving of it. Damn it, I'm going to Chicago. And then Hawaii. With Jake."

Chapter Thirty-six

During August, Sarah donated some of her time working with the committee planning the September Harvest event. There were several community gardens in the semi-rural areas of the city, sponsored by one of the local nurseries. A number of community groups planted and worked the gardens all spring and summer and in September the culmination of their efforts was the harvest of all the vegetables to be cleaned and frozen for use in the community kitchens during the early winter months. It was a major coordination effort of digging, hauling, cleaning, prepping and packaging the vegetables then transporting them to various freezers around the city in a timely manner to preserve their nutrition value. Her job was to help coordinate the volunteers and secure the sorting locations.

She was familiar with many of the community centres in the downtown area that could provide the tables and workspace needed. Not all the halls were available on the days the trucks and manpower were so it took many phone calls, trips to inspect locations, et cetera. One evening she was on foot making her way back to her condo when she spotted a man with a familiar gait near her building. He was walking away from her toward the market area. She tried calling out but didn't know his name. "Hey you" just didn't seem to be catching his attention. A red light kept her from crossing the intersection and before she knew it, he had rounded a corner and was out of sight. She hurried across the street as soon as she could but he was gone.

It was the first time she had caught sight of him and was surprised that it was so close to her home. Had he been looking for her? She was certain he knew her building but it had been dark and cold and maybe one doorway looked the same as another to a freezing man on a dark frigid night. Maybe he had business in her neighbourhood. She looked around and realized that was unlikely as there were only a couple of small bistros on the block and a pharmacy on one corner. She went upstairs to her condo and drew a bath to relax her aching feet. She had pounded a lot of pavement that day. When travelling to somewhere it's easy to forget that one has to return that same distance. The fact that she had crisscrossed several blocks added to the distance covered.

Helen called later to confirm her promise of help to sort and pack vegetables on the day in question. Sarah was relieved as several of her regulars had backed off for various reasons and they were short of workers.

After a late snack of cold cuts and pasta salad she slipped into her pyjamas and poured a glass of wine. The evening national news was just starting when she settled on the sofa. After listening to some of the international stories she was about to turn it off and go to bed when the local news headline announced a drive-by shooting just hours ago in a downtown neighbourhood. One man was dead and another was seriously injured and taken to hospital. A description of the vehicle was given and no reason for the shooting was known.

Shootings in the downtown area, while happening occasionally, had not been a common occurrence this summer. It had been a relatively quiet crime scene this tourist season. Sarah wondered what had prompted it and hoped that the victims were not just innocent bystanders. The timing of the shooting could very well have been in the timeframe she was out on the streets herself. The thought sent a shiver through her. *No one is safe.*

The morning news brought no new developments or updates on the shootings. The names of the victims were not revealed, nor was the shooter identified. It was Saturday so she had no reason to go outside which meant she could try a new tart recipe she had seen on Facebook.

Around noon, she got a call from Gordon. He and Gracie had returned from New York the week before. Gracie had enjoyed her time with her grandparents and seemed to have suffered no ill effects from staying in the apartment she and her mother had lived in for most of her life. Sarah had been so relieved to learn this after some of the trauma Gracie had suffered in settling in to her new home in Montreal.

"So what's going on in Ottawa with that shooting, Mom?"

"Nothing that I'm aware of. I guess it must have made national news if you know about it in Montreal. It'll probably be written off as drug related until the shooter is found and maybe proven to be otherwise."

"I guess the guy who was taken to hospital almost bled out. I was called to give a blood donation last night. I understand they didn't have enough in the blood bank for him."

"You haven't had to do that for a while. Wow. He's lucky you were available."

"Yeah, well, that's the price of having a rare blood type. It's good to know there are others around in case I ever need it." One time when Gordie had needed surgery, his pre-op test showed that his blood type was not common and he had to give a couple pints of his own blood to the hospital ahead of the surgery just in case. Since then, he had been called upon from time to time when his blood type was needed.

"What are you up to this morning? I know you're working hard for the harvest."

"I don't do volunteering on weekends if I can help it. I want to try a new tart recipe today and I may see if Olivia or Stella wants to go out for supper."

"Have you heard from Jake lately?"

"He's in an old timers' golf tournament this weekend so I don't expect to hear much from him until next week."

"Gracie's marking the weeks on the calendar until you guys come up again."

"How are her piano lessons coming along?"

"Pretty good. She likes the teacher we found. The woman is more into pop music than classical so she loves that."

"The women here are worried about Jake's promise to take her white-water rafting. They think he's a little old and out of shape for that."

"Mom, Jake's probably in better shape than I am. If he lost a few pounds he could probably run a marathon. How are your plans for Hawaii coming along? I understand you're going to fly out of Chicago."

"It will save a lot of flying and driving back and forth. I think we're going to spend a week or so on Oahu and another week on Maui. That should give us our fill of beaches, golf courses and volcanoes."

"I hope you guys have fun. "

"Thank you. First, I want to test the waters in Toronto. It's time I visited your sister and saw my grandsons. I'm way overdue for that and then we have to make sure Gracie gets her fill of fishing. Is there anything I can cook, bring or buy?"

"Nothing. Absolutely nothing. We're just looking forward to spending some time with you guys again. It's such a relaxing way for me to spend time away from the office. I think Gracie would give anything to move to Ottawa just to be closer to you."

"It's an idea, son. You can work from anywhere you choose and I would love for both of you to be closer to me."

"I'll give it some thought and I'm happy you are thinking of visiting Emily. I know it's not easy for either of you."

Chapter Thirty-seven

The conversation with Emily proved more difficult than Sarah had anticipated. She knew it wasn't going to be easy but was surprised by the tack it took. It was devastating. The relationship between the two women had always been strained. Emily had always let her mother know how much she had felt neglected and always given second place to her brother. She had not wanted, actually resented, advice from her financial adviser brother on how to handle her money, especially so when her mother had suggested it, and instead chose to go in her own direction. The situation had worsened over the years instead of getting better. Sarah rarely was invited to see her grandsons and when she insisted, there were always reasons why it couldn't happen when convenient for her. True to form, Emily was going to be busy well into September, plus she and her husband had travel plans of their own for October. She told her mother to call whenever she returned from her vacation and maybe they could work something out then. When Sarah attempted to push for an earlier date, Emily's tone grew quite chilly.

"Mother, I don't know why you are so insistent on trying to recapture a relationship that was never there in the first place."

"Emily, what do you mean?"

"You know exactly what I mean, Mother. I mean that when I was a child and needed you, you weren't there. You shoved me off on to whoever could or would look after me. Then when you met another man, you conveniently found the time to stay home and look after his child. By then I was out of your hair in school all day. But he was barely cold in the grave when you found another man. I do have to say you chose well. Harold was at least kind to me. Not like Gordon who only had eyes for his own son. Harold gave me the love that you didn't and he made me feel wanted. Then when he died, you felt my brother should step in and look after everything, even the inheritance I received. As if my husband and I couldn't do that on our own. It was always Gordon can help you with this and Gordon can help you with that. Well, I didn't need his help. We didn't need his help. We've managed quite nicely on our own. I didn't need Gordon and I don't need you. You are welcome to see your grandsons but I'm not sure they feel the same need you do. We'll discuss it when you're finished travelling with your new man. I believe this is number four? Really, Mother, you're getting a bit old to still be husband hunting. Call me when you get back in October."

♥ ♥ ♥

Sarah sat with the receiver in her hand for a good fifteen minutes. The steady *beep beep beep* signalling the close of the call finally alerted her to hang up the phone. She was too stunned even to cry. She knew that Emily had always felt Sarah had neglected her but she hadn't realized it had grown into such a devastating, destructive, overwhelming force. It was almost venomous. She sat staring at the floor. *What have I done? How could I have let this level of hatred materialize? Dear God, what can I do?*

♥ ♥ ♥

When Sarah hadn't answered her door or her phone by late afternoon the next day, Margaret let herself in with a key. The four women had made an agreement years before to do this if they ever felt one of them might be in distress. She found Sarah sitting on her balcony with a cold cup of coffee in front of her and staring out over the city. She approached her friend quietly and placed a hand on her shoulder.

"Why do we do it, Margaret? Why do we insist on having children when maybe we shouldn't? Do they even get an opportunity to ask if they want to be born? No. And even if they did, maybe we're not the mother they want. Maybe they'd be happier being someone else's child."

"Something tells me you've been talking to Emily."

Sarah turned to Margaret. "Is it that obvious? Is it only me that hasn't been aware how much my daughter hates me?" Tears were streaming down her cheeks.

"Sarah, Emily doesn't hate you."

"Well, you didn't hear the conversation we had. There's no other word for the feelings she's developed for me. Unless it's despise. Maybe despise is more accurate than hate."

"Tell me what happened, Sarah."

Sarah repeated the conversation. Speaking as if from a distant place, she managed to tell the whole story. Margaret took her friend's cold hand. She wrapped her arms around Sarah's shoulders and stood her up.

"Let's go inside and I'll make you some fresh coffee. First, I'll let the others know you're okay."

After about ninety minutes of talking, crying and even some humour, Sarah was able to look her friend in the eye. "I honestly thought I was doing the best I could. When Tom walked out and his parents wouldn't accept the fact the baby was their son's, I was completely on my own. My mother helped out with babysitting when she could but she had a job too. I had to work two jobs just to pay for daycare and make ends meet. But it's not just me Emily is resentful toward. It's Gordon, her stepdad. She thinks he cared more for his son than he did for her. Of course that's only natural but he was so good to her. He was kind and caring but she didn't seem to see that. She became belligerent and testy, always competing for Gordon's attention. When he was killed and the insurance money allowed me to stay home to care for Junior instead of sending him to daycare she took that to mean I loved him more than her. I stayed home with him but not with her."

"Sarah, you have to realize she doesn't have only your blood and personality, she has her dad's as well. It seems like he might have been spoiled, not taught to face up to responsibility. She may have inherited some of those personality traits. You mentioned how she loved Harold. He treated both of your children equally. He loved them both equally. She didn't have to compete with her brother for attention. He gave her away like a real father at her wedding. He was there for her every step of the way. He was grandfather to her sons. She provided him with grandchildren, something that Gordie didn't do. Then when he died, it was back to her and Gordie sharing your love again. The difference is she had her own family and your son was the head of your family. You relied on him and trusted him. Not her. She wasn't needed anymore."

Sarah listened and began to understand. She marvelled that Margaret had seen all this and understood Emily completely. "I have a lot of repair work to do. I can see that now. Thank you, Margaret."

"If I were you, I would leave it alone until the fall when she's expecting you to call again. Give her the space she needs. She may do some soul searching in the meantime and realize some of her words were unnecessarily cruel and wish to take them back. Don't blame her, Sarah, and above all, don't blame yourself. You've both been victims of circumstance."

Sarah nodded. "Like I said, maybe babies should be asked if they want to be born and to whom."

"I bet Emily, given the opportunity, would say yes to you. Maybe not yes to having a brother but yes to you as a mother." Margaret gave her friend a long warm hug and left.

Chapter Thirty-eight

Sarah joined Margaret and Helen for lunch later that week in the market. It was a beautiful August day, warm sunshine without humidity. They were seated at a corner table watching the many tourists lined up at a food wagon across the way when a man moved in front of the window blocking their view. He was standing with his back to them so close that Helen could have reached up and touched him had it not been for the glass between them. She commented on what nice hair he had. The others looked up. Sarah was out of her chair in a flash and making her way to the door.

She was out on the street just in time to see the man starting to walk away. She quickened her pace and caught his arm. Her friends witnessed this with open mouths.

"What's she doing?" Helen was laughing. "She's taken to picking up strange men on the street."

Margaret frowned. "He doesn't appear to want to be picked up."

They watched as the startled man backed away from Sarah, looking around as if for an escape route. Margaret rose from her chair but Helen caught her arm and suggested they watch this play out. It was broad daylight and Sarah seemed to know the man.

"I've been trying to find you." Sarah looked at the man who obviously was not happy to see her.

"Look, lady. I don't know what you want but this is not a good time for a conversation."

"I just want to help you if I can."

"Help me with what? You don't know me from Adam and I don't need help, from you or anyone else." He was becoming agitated.

"I …"

"Lady, I'm going to walk away now and I want you to go back to wherever you came from. This is not a good time. Just let me be."

He started to walk away. Something in the way he moved caught Sarah's attention.

"You have been injured."

He turned abruptly. "Just go away. Now."

"Come and see me at the soup kitchen on Wednesday. Please. I must talk to you."

She watched as he limped away. Something about him told her that he was the gunshot victim for whom Gordon had to donate blood.

♥ ♥ ♥

"Why would you think that?" Margaret was perplexed by Sarah's explanation of why she had accosted the man in the street.

"Every now and again, I get a feeling that I should know him. I don't think it's a coincidence that he and Gordon have the same blood."

"Do you think he singled out your doorway on purpose last winter?"

"I don't know. I don't think so. He doesn't seem to know me or even want to know me."

"You don't really think he's going to show up on Wednesday, do you?" Helen looked sceptical.

"Probably not, but I couldn't just let him walk away. He

seemed afraid of something or someone."

"Maybe he's involved with drugs and is afraid whoever took a shot at him the other night might try it again."

"Really, Margaret, I think you're reading more into this than is necessary. The police said they felt the injured man was an innocent victim caught in crossfire. I think he doesn't want me to find out who he is for another reason."

"Like what?"

"I have no idea. Let's wait and see if he shows up on Wednesday."

Helen suggested that maybe she should go with Sarah that day just in case.

"In case of what?"

"Sarah, you are not yourself. You seem mesmerized by this man and I'm not sure you're thinking rationally. What will you do if he shows up? Bring him home? Follow him? Where do you think all this is going to lead? How is it going to end?"

The three women looked at each other in silence.

"I don't know where or how it's going to end." Sarah stared off into space for several moments. "You know when he looked at me from behind those blankets last winter, it seemed like those eyes were seeing into my very soul. I was numb. When he limped away, I felt like I had been tested and I had failed. Miserably."

Margaret and Helen exchanged glances. They knew how deeply their friend felt things.

"I know he's in my life for a reason. If not, I would never have seen him again. Our paths would not have crossed again and again. I must find out why."

❣ ❣ ❣

He did not come to the kitchen on Wednesday. She had watched and studied everyone who came through the door, disappointed with each passing moment. He was, however, waiting outside the entrance to her parkade when she drove home. She stopped short of her entrance and he slowly made his way to her car and spoke to her through the opened window.

"I don't know what you want from me but I can see something is on your mind. I'll wait for you in the bistro next door." He walked away without waiting for her to reply.

Sarah quickly parked her car then took the elevator to street level. She almost bowled Gerald Mercier over as she rushed through the foyer from the elevator to the street.

"What the —? Sarah. Where are you off to in such a hurry?"

"I can't talk right now, Gerald. I'll call later." She was through the door before he could respond.

She spotted the man sitting at a table with his back to the door near the rear of the small restaurant and slid onto the chair opposite.

"You really don't like being seen, do you?"

She was relieved to see him smile. He had a pleasant face. She guessed him to be maybe ten years or so her junior. His dark eyes were fastened on hers.

"I figure you're not going to give me any rest until we talk. I don't know what's so important to you about me but let's get it over with."

Finally confronted with the opportunity to get to know the man, Sarah didn't know where to start. She ordered a cup of tea and sat back in her chair. It seemed anticlimactic that this conversation should take place in such a mundane place as a small bistro next door to where she had encountered him eight months earlier.

Chapter Thirty-nine

"Can I start by asking your name?"

"Bob. You told me yours was Sarah."

"Bob what?"

He hesitated then offered. "Archer. Robert Archer."

It was not familiar to Sarah.

"I'm Sarah Eisenboch."

He shrugged.

"Where are you from Robert Archer?"

"Here, originally. I lived away for a while but settled back here many years ago."

"Are you living on the street?"

He let out a long breath, almost a sigh. "No."

He shifted in his seat slightly. "Why do you want to know about me?"

"As I told you before, I was filled with guilt when I didn't offer you warmth or shelter or even a hot cup of coffee that night in front of my building. I …"

"I told you not to feel guilty. I thought all you wanted was to apologize and you did. I accepted that. You seemed like a nice lady and I'm not one to hold a grudge."

"You have come a long way since that night. You are clean and tidy, nicely dressed, appear to be well-nourished. I've noticed you a few times around the market since then. Once you were still dressed rather raggedly and appeared unkempt but since then you appear quite … quite …"

"Normal?" He smiled.

"Yes. Quite normal." Sarah sipped her tea. "What's your story, Robert? And why were you nervous about being seen with me on the street the other day?"

"I prefer Bob if you don't mind."

"Bob."

"There are several reasons why I didn't want you near me that day. One is that I was accidentally shot a short while ago and I don't know why or by whom so I don't feel completely safe on the street. Even though the police released to the press that I was not the target in the shooting, I believe they are keeping an eye on me to make sure of that. I've noticed a heavier than usual presence of them in the market and they always seem to have me in their line of vision."

"And the other reason?"

"I don't want to give the people living on the street any reason to believe I am not who they think I am."

This startled Sarah. "If you're not who they think you are, then who are you?"

"I'm Bob Archer. They know me as Sam. Or the book guy. Or the gimp. Some call me Blacky because of my dark eyes."

Sarah studied his face. She tried picturing him with different coloured eyes but he just faded. His eyes were his prominent feature. It had been his eyes that drew her to him in the first place.

"What's your story?"

His question surprised her.

"My story? I'm afraid I don't have one."

"Then why the interest in me? I'm just another street person. You must see us all over the place and not really give us too much thought."

"That's just it. I don't know why I'm so interested in you.

There's something about you that seems familiar somehow. I feel like I should know you but I don't. What part of the city did you grow up in?"

"The west end. Nepean area."

"Hmm. I'm not too familiar with any place west of Bank Street. When did you take to the streets?"

"Last winter."

"Last winter." He just recently fell on hard times she thought. Maybe just a temporary thing? "What did you do before that?"

He seemed reluctant to answer.

"Look, I know what it's like to have to stretch a dollar. Maybe work two jobs to make ends meet. There's no shame in that."

"You?" He motioned to the neighbourhood in general. "I hardly think you've had to look too far for your next meal."

"There was a time, believe me." She rolled her spoon over and over. "If it wasn't for having a child to care for, I may have been on the street myself. I guess that's why I have a compassion for those not as lucky as I."

"What happened?"

"I was fortunate to meet a wonderful man who fell in love with me and was happy to raise my daughter as his own and gave me a son to love as well."

"And you've lived happily ever after."

"Not exactly. He died. I was blessed that he left me better off than he found me. I've tried to share some of my good fortune with others ever since."

She looked at the man across the table from her. "You now know more about me than I know about you. You should think about doing interviews for a living as you seem to have the knack of drawing people out. You did the same at the shelter when I first met you. You sat patiently and waited for me to do all the talking."

Bob smiled ruefully. "I was an only child. I never knew my father and my mother died when I was twenty-seven years old. She provided well for me. I never wanted for anything, including a good education. That's why the people on the street call me the book guy. They think I must read a lot because I appear to be better educated than most of them. I moved away from Ottawa while I was in university and lived in southern Ontario for a while after graduating. I lived in Vancouver for a number of years before coming back here. Ottawa has been my home most of my life."

"What have you done for a living?"

"I've worked mostly in human relations. Public service work."

"What happened last winter?"

"I was in a position that necessitated my taking to the streets for a while." He seemed uncomfortable talking about it.

"You seem to have pulled yourself together again."

"You might say that."

Sarah broached the subject that was bothering her. "You bled rather seriously from your gunshot wound, I understand."

"How would you know that?" His back straightened.

"My son was called to give blood. He lives in Montreal and was told there was a desperate need for his rare type in Ottawa. The news reports said there was an unusual amount of blood at the scene of the second man's injury."

"It seems I owe your son a thank you."

"When I tried talking to you outside the restaurant in the market last week, I saw that you were in some pain, and just barely made out the bandage through your T-shirt. You were very jumpy and kept looking around as if you were waiting for someone to attack you. It was easy to put two and two together.

"Bob, I think it's more than coincidence that we've crossed paths more than once. I think there's a reason for it and that's what I'm trying desperately to find out. I think you're holding something back from me. You're not being completely honest with me and I don't know why."

He looked her directly in the eye. "You're right, Sarah. I haven't been completely honest with you but not in the way you think. I promise to come straight with you soon but you will have to trust me for a little while yet. Unlike you, I do think it's coincidence that has brought us together, nothing more. I think you may be able to help with something but I'm just not quite there yet."

"So you'll stay in touch?"

"Yes, I will."

"Where can I reach you?"

"You can't. That's part of the trust I'm asking for."

"You're asking that all the trust be on my side."

"I know, but it has to be that way. Believe me when I say, I mean you no harm. I owe your son my life and I won't ever forget that. Now I have to go."

He stood and abruptly walked out of the bistro leaving Sarah once again with more questions than answers.

Chapter Forty

"Are you out of your mind, Sarah? You told him who you are without knowing anything about him? You don't even know if he gave you his real name. He also knows where you live and you have no idea what fleabag room he might call home."

"Helen, I never knew you to be such a snob!"

"I'm sorry, but he's a person living on the streets who is playing at your heart strings. Maybe your purse strings. Have you thought about that, Sarah? Anyone who knows you knows how generous you are. You are a sucker for a sob story. He's going to fleece you, sure as anything."

"Helen is right, Sarah." Olivia jumped into the conversation. "He's an example of those scammers that entice women on the Internet to trust them by feigning friendship and hardship. They start out slowly then gradually raise the ante. He'll play on your sympathy until you're so wrapped up in his needs you'll give him anything."

Sarah couldn't believe her ears. "You two are being so melodramatic. I can't believe what you're saying. He's asked me for nothing."

"He's asked for your absolute trust."

"Gerald, are you turning on me too?"

He touched her elbow. "Sarah, listen to reason. Just promise us that you will not give him any money no matter what kind of story he gives you. Women with your trust in human nature are vulnerable."

Sarah had stopped at Helen and Gerald's to apologize for ignoring him so rudely in the foyer earlier. She had wanted to share the conversation she'd had with Bob and was astounded at the reaction it had triggered.

She had wanted to call Gordon and tell him that she had met the recipient of his blood donation but had second thoughts. *He'll jump all over me too no doubt.* She laughed to herself. *And he has my power of attorney.*

Instead, she poured herself a glass of wine and chose to listen to The Eagles while she read the newspaper she had left on the kitchen table that morning. The only news that caught her eye was a write-up about the police catching the shooter from the incident in which Bob had been injured. Too bad she hadn't seen that before her conversation with him.

His request for her trust really seemed to have her friends' backs up. He hadn't asked for money or anything else. Only trust. Well, that she could give him. Maybe not many people had given him even that even though he had said that his mother had provided well for him. She would have to wait to hear the rest of his story but at least he had given her his background. His mother sounded like she might have gone through a situation similar to Sarah's. She guessed that he had respected his mother more than Sarah's daughter had respected her. She pondered uselessly how she might have done things differently with Emily.

♥ ♥ ♥

"Hi, darlin'. What a nice surprise."

"I was sitting here wishing I could feel your arm around my shoulder."

"I can probably be there by morning if I drive fast."

Jake could always make her laugh, no matter how down her mood was. "You probably would too if I asked. That's what makes you so you, Jakub Tatarek."

"It's always nice to know you are thinking about me."

She realized she had been thinking about him more and more. Chicago had never seemed so far away before. In fact she had never given much thought to Jake or Chicago until early winter when it was time to make plans for Florida. Her summers in Ottawa had always been busy between her various committees, golfing, and playing bridge. Now she seemed to have a void that wasn't there before.

"I was thinking about you and wondering what you're up to."

"I was out car shopping today. I'm not sure my old wheels will get me to Florida this year. Time to trade them in."

"What are you looking at?"

"I've been reading up on the electric cars and maybe leaning toward one of them."

"I thought you were going to say you were looking at station wagons."

His laughter took a while to die.

"Is that how I really appear to you, darlin'? A station wagon kind of guy?"

"I guess not. I know for a fact you're pretty techy so I shouldn't be surprised you know all about the cars of the future." She smiled. "Did I tell you that my car still has a CD player?"

"I did notice that when I was there but was too polite to say anything."

She marvelled at how easy the conversation drifted from one thing to another. He was easier to talk with than her friends. The realization that forty-five minutes had slipped by surprised her. She wasn't anywhere near ready to say goodbye when they terminated the call. She had wanted to tell him about her conversation with Emily. She had wanted to tell him about her conversation with Robert Archer. She had wanted to, but didn't.

Maybe I'm really not so ready for you, Mr. Tatarek.

❦ ❦ ❦

The next morning she delved back into her work with the garden harvest. One day followed the next and a week had gone by when her buzzer rang at lunch time one day. It was Bob calling from the foyer. She invited him up.

"This is a surprise." She greeted him at her door hoping that no one had seen him on his way up.

"I hadn't intended talking to you again so soon but something has come up." He followed her through to the kitchen.

A pang of concern gripped her stomach. Was this going to be the start of a shakedown? Were her friends right about him?

"Oh?" She wasn't sure what more to say.

He looked out her kitchen window at the skyline beyond. "You have a beautiful view of the city."

"Yes. It's always changing. It seems every time I look out, another building is going up. Ottawa is growing." She motioned for him to sit at the table. "I was just about to make a sandwich. Can I make one for you as well?"

"Sure. That would be nice."

She placed a sandwich and a mug of coffee in front of him then returned to the refrigerator for cream. It wasn't until she sat with her food in front of her and lifted her sandwich to her mouth that he bit into his own. The good manners didn't go unnoticed. He had been well-trained in proper etiquette. This man was not accustomed to a life on the street. Of grabbing what you could before someone else got to it first. She saw how the hungry who came for meals at the shelter were more concerned with filling their empty bellies than waiting until everyone was seated at the table. It made her wonder more about what his story was.

"I guess you're wondering what brings me here today."

"I'm curious, yes."

"I've reached a point where your help would be most beneficial to my project."

She felt the lump in her throat as she swallowed. "Help? What kind of help are you looking for?"

Please don't ask for money. Please. Please.

"I've not been honest with you, although you've probably already surmised that." He took the last bite of his sandwich and washed it down with coffee before he looked at her and continued. "I have been doing some research and I need your viewpoint before I can go on."

"What kind of research have you been doing?"

"I've been studying the homeless in Ottawa for eight months now. I am concluding my research as a victim and now I have to shift my focus to those who help them."

"You said 'them', not 'us'."

He hesitated and toyed with the corners of his napkin.

"I'm sorry for misleading you. I am not homeless. I have gone undercover so to speak and been living among them all this time."

Sarah sat back and studied the man in front of her. He was aware of her scrutiny and allowed her to give him a careful once-over with both her eyes and her thoughts.

"Is Robert Archer even your real name?"

"Yes. Everything I've told you about me is true except I have a job and a home."

"Okay. Then it's time for you to fess up and give me the real story."

"I came today prepared to do just that." He smiled and asked if he might have another cup of coffee before he got into it.

He started out by reassuring her that he had never seen her before that cold night in January. When he had curled up in her entryway, it was only because that seemed like a good spot to do so. The cement had been swept clean of snow so it was dry and it offered shelter from the wind. That was only his second night of actually being out on the street in the extreme cold. He had found the dirty, smelly old blankets in a bin behind one of the shelters. His clothes underneath were actually his own. Only the outer layers were foul smelling.

"Why were you doing this? For what purpose?"

"I have a Masters Degree in psychology, specializing in human behaviour. I've been working on my PhD programme for a very long time and finally had the funds available that I needed to take my research to the street. I wanted to experience homelessness in its most raw form so I could write and react to it from my own existence at that level."

Sarah let all this sink in. He was not a homeless person. He was well-educated, living and working under funding of some kind. She had suspected there was more to him than what was apparent to passers-by on the street. But this? She was completely thrown. Questions popped into her head. So many questions.

Two hours of questions and answers later, her phone rang.

"Hey, Sarah, I'm going to the east end for some sausages. Do you want to come for the ride?"

It was Olivia. She had found a Polish butcher who made his own sausages and salamis. They all loved his meats but today was not the day. Sausage shopping suddenly felt mundane. How could she possibly concentrate on kolbasa when this mystery that had consumed much of her thoughts over the past year was unravelling in front of her?

"Not today, Olivia. Thanks, but I'm involved with a project that I want to stay with. I'll talk to you later."

Bob apologized for taking up so much of her time.

"I'd best let you get back to your own projects. I understand you are heavily involved in the community garden harvest."

"I'm sure there isn't much going on downtown that you're not aware of, Bob."

"Sarah, as you are now well aware, I must keep what I'm doing under my hat for a little while longer. I have to ask you to maintain a complete silence about everything we've discussed. I have a few more interviews to do before I can complete my report. You may know some of the people I want to talk to and I don't want their views skewed. As I explained, the actions and reactions of some people are very different depending on who they think they're talking to. I need honest answers and honest feedbacks if this study is going to provide the information I'm hoping to bring forward. I had thought each neighbourhood would respond differently because of different income levels, but I was surprised by how varied the reactions were inside of each regardless of income."

"I understand, Bob. I have so many more questions but I have enough to digest already. My head is spinning. I will respect your need for privacy and complete confidentiality. This is certainly not the outcome I had anticipated from all my worry and concern about shunning you last January." She shook her head and couldn't hold back a mild laugh. "I still have this niggling feeling that there's more to this than what's on the surface."

"I've been completely honest with you."

"I trust you. I just think there's more to this than either of us is aware of."

Chapter Forty-one

He gave her his cell phone number, cautioning her to text only, not call. He didn't tell her where he was staying or give any other identifying information. The only physical contact was the handshake he extended as he departed. She hoped he wouldn't meet any of her friends before exiting onto the street. They would be relentless in their questioning if any spotted him in her vicinity after having seen him near the restaurant.

❣ ❣ ❣

The next week went by quickly. The fishing trip, Hawaiian vacation, and harvest plans all were moving along well. Gracie and Jake were the major planners of the fishing expedition leaving Gordon and Sarah to look after the incidentals such as food and camping supplies. They were fortunate enough to have access to the same cabin they had occupied in June.

Jacob had an excellent travel agent within his circle of friends so the Hawaii arrangements were moving along right on schedule. Her passport was up to date. That and her travel wardrobe seemed to be her only responsibility there. So that left her only to deal with the harvest.

Pickers, trucks, warehouse space, food preppers, and freezer space all seemed to be on track.

She hadn't heard from nor seen Bob since his enlightening visit to her apartment. Her life seemed to be on hold these days, knowing that "things" were going to happen soon but nothing more would be done about anything in the immediate future.

Gracie had assured her that a white-water rafting was definitely going to happen. She had been attending to her piano lessons and practices without fail and even had a special surprise planned for Jake. *White-water rafting will be a duo expedition with Gracie and Jake as the sole family members in that boat.* She hoped hitting golf balls every day was enough exercise to keep his arms muscled for guiding a rubber raft through turbulent water. She knew the rafting companies had all safety precautions well taken care of and had never heard nor read about any drownings concerning rafters in the news. She was confident the two would be safe. It was just one experience in which she didn't care to participate. When it would happen wasn't clear but it would have to be between the fishing trip and their departure for Hawaii. October would be too cold for an enjoyable water adventure, especially one that promised a good soaking.

♥ ♥ ♥

She and a group of volunteers were at one of the community centres making sure all the supplies were in place for the arrival of the harvested vegetables the next day, when her phone beeped. It was Bob. "Are you free to meet with me tomorrow for a couple of hours?"

"I am tied up with the harvest for the whole day. I have to oversee all the locations to make sure the vegetables are cleaned, packaged and delivered to the freezers on schedule."

"I'll get back to you about an alternate date."

She didn't receive anything else from him for several days. Labour Day was behind her and all her community work was finished for the time being. Gracie and Gordon had spent the long weekend with her and the girl had enjoyed some time with her new friend, Kelly. Jake would be arriving at the end of the following week for the fishing trip so Sarah was enjoying some downtime. No responsibilities. No appointments. Two of her close friends had gone away on short trips to visit family. Nothing but free time and beautiful September sunshine.

Her phone rang while she was watching the evening news.

"Are you free to meet me this evening?"

"Hi, Bob. Well, I have nothing on my plate. Do you want to come here?"

"If that's okay with you. I can be there in ten minutes."

He declined an offer of a glass of wine, opting for a soft drink.

"Do you not drink alcohol?"

"I have the occasional beer. I experienced a severe reaction to red wine once so I avoid them all."

Sarah closed her hands over the goosebumps on her arms and felt a slight chill. She turned the television off and set her Anker speaker to some soft classical music. Bob recognized the composer which indicated at least some hint of a musical background. She commented on this.

He smiled. "My mother was always aware of no male influences in my life so she made sure I was always enrolled in activities that included male coaches and instructors. I played hockey, soccer, rowed on the high school rowing team, et cetera. But she also wanted me to appreciate the arts as well so she ..." He stopped and took time for a brief chuckle. Sarah noticed the soft, wistful look in his eyes. "She searched until she found a male music teacher who had also been a star athlete until an injury forced him to give up sports and hone his musical abilities. She didn't want my lack of a father or siblings to detract me from my full potential whatever road I chose."

"She sounds like a devoted mother."

"She was and she always let me know that it was through the kindness of my father that she had the monetary means to allow me these paths."

"I envy her. I was a single mother for a number of years but was forced to work long hours to provide for my daughter and me. She always resented the time I didn't spend with her. I can't blame her, it wasn't easy for her but she's a middle-aged adult now and still having trouble forgiving."

"I'm sorry to hear that."

"We're working on it but I'm afraid it's a long work in progress." She smiled and directed the conversation back to his reason for being there.

He took a couple swallows from his glass and asked permission to record their conversation, assuring her it would not be heard by anyone but him. He explained that he had completed his studies of the homeless at the street level and now he was examining the thoughts, concerns and actions about the homelessness of the people not living in poverty. After an hour or so of questions regarding her philanthropic activities and her attitude toward the less fortunate, he asked about the night they had first encountered each other.

He motioned to her surroundings. "You obviously are not living pay cheque to pay cheque. You have a beautiful home many levels above the street below where you encountered a man seeking shelter in your doorway." He waved away her attempt to respond.

"I'm not judging you. I have found that your initial response to my being there was typical of people of your station in life. What isn't typical is your feelings following it."

The interview followed his tack of letting her take her time with her answers. He sat listening while she talked. She found for the first time since it had happened that she was allowed to let all her feelings out. He was the first person to whom she had ever given insight to her personal wealth. Gordon, her lawyer, and the Canada Revenue Agency were the only ones privy to her investments and income. She also told this stranger how guilty she felt about it all and he didn't try to assuage this guilt.

Suddenly she realized she had been going on for over an hour and this man was now the only other person on earth who was privy to what was contained in her very soul. She looked up at him and searched his eyes.

He turned the recorder off. "If there were more people like you in this world, Sarah Eisenboch, there would be no homeless people."

"I'm not sure that's true, Bob. I keep thinking about that eye of the needle my camel has to pass through before I can reap any reward."

"After nine months of living on the streets, I can tell you that you are closer to it than anyone I've met." He stood. "I know you've probably told me more tonight than anyone in your family or circle of friends knows about you and I thank you for that. You will remain as an anonymous donor to my research unless you allow me to use your name in my list of acknowledgements. No mention of any information you have given me will ever accompany your name, only that you donated some insight."

"I prefer to remain anonymous unless it adds to the credence of your work."

"I will let you know and get your written permission if I find the need to include it."

"What happens now?"

"Now I have a few more interviews with people working in this industry to conduct, then compiling, writing, editing and submitting all the information and my conclusions. About another six to ten months of work."

"You are not a young man, why did you decide to do this at your age?"

He laughed. "I've had a blessed life also. When I listened to peoples' stories in my line of work, I became curious about the how and why of the homeless. I wanted to learn the reason for the numbers of homeless growing while our economy was supposedly booming. Why so many people were falling between the cracks while income levels were on the rise. I was curious about the statistics comparing cities with the highest median of family income to the rate of homelessness. I chose Ottawa as the base for my research after sitting in the Market one day and observing the vast range of people coming and going. I returned in the evening to see if there was any change in the demographics of the daytime and nighttime crowds."

"Were you not afraid you would be recognized?"

"Actually, I was heavily bearded and long-haired in my regular life. By shaving both my hair and my face I was almost unrecognizable. Once the cold weather eased, I let my hair grow a bit and usually had a bit of stubble on my face. My friends and colleagues think I'm in Australia studying down there."

"Will you come out of hiding now?"

"Soon. I'll let you know when you can tell your son and your friends they don't have to worry about you anymore."

"Speaking about my son, I would like for the two of you to meet. I'd love for him to know the man whose life he saved is using it to improve the fate of so many others."

"I'd like that."

"Do you mind me asking what caused your limp?"

"I was injured while serving in Bosnia in the '90s. It's when I was in the armed forces that I found out I had a rare blood type." He smiled. "That's why I chose a desk job, trying to stay away from trouble because of it. I never thought I'd ever take a bullet walking down a street in my home town."

Chapter Forty-two

"What do you mean they're moving to Ottawa?"

"I'm as surprised as you are, believe me."

Her friends' smiling faces lit up the table where they were playing their bridge game. Sarah had received a Facetime call from Gracie the evening before, telling her their news. Apparently, the girl had experienced some difficulty settling into school again. She seemed to be having difficulty finding friends with whom she felt a bond. She was feeling lonely and was sinking into a mild depression. Gordon had noticed that she wasn't eating well and he could hear her moving around in her room late at night. They discussed what might bring her some happiness and she answered without any hesitation. "Moving to Ottawa where Grandma is."

This had been chatted about rather vaguely a few times between Sarah and her son so when Gracie voiced a strong desire for it to happen, Gordon didn't hesitate in agreeing to his daughter's request.

"Apparently, they're going to put their place in Montreal on the market and will start looking for a suitable home here. They're hoping they can be settled in for Christmas so that Gracie can start the January school semester here."

Margaret grabbed Sarah's hand and squeezed. "You must be tickled pink."

Sarah eyed them all and sighed. "If I had been told last March that this would ever be possible, I never would have believed it. When they came to visit me in Florida, Gracie was very distant and cool. I got the feeling she could hardly wait to leave. It was Jake who salvaged that vacation. I … I …" The moisture started spilling from her eyes. "I can't believe how much things have changed in these last six or seven months."

"And they'll change even more over the next three or four." Olivia smiled kindly at Sarah. "Nobody deserves some happiness in her life more than you, my friend. You are always the one worrying about everyone else and in the meantime your own life has become a real roller coaster. I have a feeling this winter is going to see it level out at the top of the ride."

Sarah wiped her eyes. "I hope you're right."

She hesitated, wondering if this was the right time to tell them the rest of her story. The call from Gracie and Gordon hadn't been the only one she had received the evening before. Bob had phoned to tell her that his research was now pretty well complete and if she chose to do so, she could tell her family and friends about his work and the relationship they had shared. She hadn't mentioned it to her family last night as their exciting news was the highlight of that call and she didn't want to detract from it. She had decided to save the conversation with Bob for another time.

"Of course she's right." Margaret smiled. "There are only happy times ahead from here until year end. Jake's coming up and you're all going fishing. Then you and Jake are going on a romantic trip to the Hawaiian Islands. By the time you get back you'll be planning your family's move to be near you and then a big Christmas dinner all together. I'll bet Jake will be here too. I see this coming New Year as one of the happiest ever."

"Now, now. Don't go jinxing things, Margaret. I'll take it one step at a time." Sarah decided her other news could wait for a day or two. It wasn't going anywhere and didn't make any difference in her life or theirs except for revealing that Bob really wasn't a street person. Besides she wanted to talk about it to Gordie first.

❣ ❣ ❣

Jake arrived the following week, happy to share in Sarah's excitement about her family moving closer. The call to Jake had been Gracie's second call, even before the one to her grandparents in New York. To Sarah's surprise, they had been quite supportive of that move. Apparently, they had not been completely happy with Gracie's move to a city and province with such a different culture. They were extremely happy to know that their granddaughter would be back among people of "her own kind". Whatever that meant.

"So tell me, darlin', what have you been doing with yourself now that you don't have all those fancy balls and galas to plan?" Jake had unpacked and was sorting through his fishing tackle on the kitchen table. "I hope you're resting up getting ready to help us haul in some big ones next week."

Sarah placed a sandwich in front of Jake and ran a hand down his arm as she joined him. "Do I feel some muscle in there? You've been working out getting in shape for your paddle down the Ottawa River, haven't you?" She laughed. "Any second thoughts about making promises you should have given more consideration to before making?"

"Sarah, my darling, I am in the best shape I've been in in years." He bent his elbow and flexed his muscle. "Feel that. You're doggone right I've been working out. I've been lifting more than woods, drivers, and beers with these arms. I promised that young lady a ride through the rapids and that's what she's gonna get. I've already got it all booked."

"Even before you know if she came through with her end of it?"

"She says she did. Says she's even got a surprise for me and if she's anything like her grandma, she's as good as her word. My travel agent looked after it for me just to make sure there were seats available." He swallowed some of the sandwich before adding, "Booked one for you too."

Sarah stood up. "Jakub Tatarek, you better not have. You know I have no intention of getting into a rubber dinghy and riding through a raging torrent of white water."

"But I'll be there to protect you."

"I'm counting on you being there to protect my granddaughter. You know I'm not keen on this whole idea in the first place."

"You know I wouldn't take that precious little girl somewhere that wasn't safe. Nobody has ever drowned on one of those little trips down the river."

"Well, the wisdom and safety of it is between you and her father but you're not including me in it. I am NOT going with you."

❣❣❣

That evening, after a glass of wine and watching the sun go down from her balcony, they sat in front of the television searching channels. Sarah took the remote from him and switched to a music channel.

"I have something I want to tell you."

"Last time a woman said something like that to me I wondered if I was about to be sorry I hadn't used a condom."

Sarah almost choked on a mouthful of wine and punched him lightly in the shoulder. When she stopped laughing she asked, "And were you? Sorry that is?"

"No. Thank God, she just wanted to tell me she was breaking up with me."

"Oh, Jake, that's what I love so much about you. You make me laugh."

"That's all? I make you laugh?"

"No. That's not all." She caressed his hand then kissed it.

"But I do have some important stuff to tell you and I need you to listen, seriously listen."

He put an arm around her shoulders and kissed her temple. "Go ahead. I'm listening. Seriously."

She spent the next two hours telling him and answering his questions about Bob.

Chapter Forty-three

"What do you mean she's in the hospital?"

Margaret's granddaughter was relaying a message from a telephone call between her and Gracie. "That's what Gracie said. 'Mrs. Eisenboch is in the emergency ward at the hospital in Pembroke.' She called me on her dad's phone."

"Why? What else did she say? Did Sarah have a heart attack or something?"

"No. She jumped into the river trying to save Jake and ended up almost drowning and she may have a broken wrist."

"Sarah jumped into the river? What about Jake? I have to call Gordon."

Gordon wasn't answering his phone so Margaret went down to Helen's condo. "Does Gerald have Jake's phone number?"

"Yes. I'll get it. Why?"

Margaret relayed the little bit of information she had, adding that Gordon didn't answer his phone but maybe Jake or someone else would answer his. That call was fruitless as well. It was about forty-five minutes later that Gordon finally returned Margaret's message. By this time, Olivia and Stella had joined Margaret and Helen. The four women were in hysterics, each one trying to talk at once.

Finally, Gordon got them to settle down and listen to him on speaker phone so that he only had to tell it once. "First of all, my mother is fine. They're going to be releasing her shortly and we'll be on our way home. Outside of being angry at himself for Mom ending up in the hospital, Jake is fine also. He went overboard at a point where that happens with regularity. They were all warned about this and told what to do if that happens but I guess Mom missed that part of the instructions and thought that Jake was going to drown. She jumped in to save him and hit her hand against a rock. She was having trouble with her arm and trying to keep herself afloat. She swallowed quite a bit of water by the time they got to her. Jake was never in any danger but she didn't know that. Anyway, they brought her to the hospital in Pembroke to be checked over and have her wrist looked at. They think it may be fractured but they're releasing her into my care and we'll have her X-rayed at the hospital in Ottawa. There's nothing serious to worry about." He laughed slightly. "I don't know who's angrier at Jake — Mom or Jake himself. Poor guy. He's having to listen to a lot of 'I told you so's.'"

♥ ♥ ♥

Gordon and Gracie were at Helen and Gerald's picking up a late supper Helen had prepared for them. Jake was trying to convince Sarah to stay in bed but she was having no part of it. She had stopped blaming Jake for all that had happened and was almost feeling sorry for having lambasted him with accusations about the whole fiasco being prevented if he hadn't come up with his lame-brained idea in the first place. It was the first time she had ever raised a voice to him and she knew it hurt him.

She placed a hand on his cheek. "I'm sorry, darling."

His head jerked up. "You must really be mad at me. You've never called me darling before."

"I've never been so scared before."

"Scared? You should be scared. You almost drowned."

"I wasn't scared for me. I saw you fly into the water and not come up. I thought you were going to die. I couldn't let that happen. I had to do something."

"So you risked your own life."

"I didn't think about that. All I thought about was getting to you."

"Ah, darlin', if you hadn't made it, I never would have forgiven myself."

"And it would have served you right, Jakub Tatarek." She drew her to him with her good hand and kissed him soundly. Then kissed him again and again.

"I'd tell you guys to get a hotel room if you weren't already in your own bed." Gordon was in the doorway. "Supper is on the table if you're up to it."

"I can bring you a tray to eat in bed." Jake was already standing and ready to move.

"No. I need to get up. I need to feel normal." Sarah looked around. "Where is Gracie?"

"She went up to tell Kelly all about her grandmother's dance with death this afternoon."

"Oh my. I'm sure I ruined her white-water rafting experience. I hope she forgives me."

"Forgive you? Are you kidding? You're her hero, Mom. You jumped in to save Jake's life. There's nothing more heroic you could ever do in her eyes. She'll be talking about this for months to come."

Gracie asked to sleep with her grandmother that night and Gordon opened the daybed in the den for himself. The next day, life returned to a somewhat normal existence. After four days at the fishing lodge and two days back in Ottawa had gone by, Sarah finally found an opportunity to sit with Gordon before he left for home and explain all the events that had occurred over the last few months involving her experiences with Robert Archer. Jake had gone golfing with Gerald and Gracie was out with Kelly.

Her son had many, many questions and showed much concern over her involvement.

"Mom, you didn't even know this guy and you let him not only into your home, but into your personal affairs. You let him know you have money."

"He's not stupid, Gordie. He could see instantly that I was not living on social assistance."

"You still took a chance. You left yourself wide open to kidnapping or blackmail."

"Blackmail me for what?"

"Okay, maybe not blackmail but you have placed yourself in danger, Mom. Have you checked out his credentials? Have you tried to find out if he is who he says he is?"

"I checked out the university he said he attended and he does have a Masters degree and has been in their employ. He's written several papers pertaining to human relations and he's been published a number of times in various journals." She looked wryly at her son. "I'm not stupid, Gordon."

"Touché. So what are you going to do now?"

"For now, nothing. I have a trip to Hawaii coming up with a man to whom I owe some attention. Jake has been more than kind to all of us, including Gracie whom he adores. I feel I owe him some kindness and time in return — all by ourselves."

"You really care for him."

"More than I realized. I've been trying to avoid a commitment to another man but he keeps getting in the way of my resolve."

"He's a good man, Mom. I like him and I think you know how Gracie feels. What does Emily feel about him? I never did ask about your visit with her."

"That's a story for another time. We put it on hold until I come back from my vacation." She breathed a sigh of relief when he didn't question her further about his sister. "You and Gracie will be here for Thanksgiving?"

"Yes. We're hoping to have a few places lined up to see with a real estate agent. I'm having a stager come in and prepare our place for showing right after the long weekend."

"Gordon, would you be okay with me inviting Bob to join us for Thanksgiving Dinner?"

He hesitated, taking in a long breath then letting it out.

"Yes. I guess so, Mom. I'd like to check him out myself." He placed a hand on her shoulder when he saw her back stiffen. "If he's half the guy you think he is, then I'm sure I'll like him too. You say he's near your age?"

"I'm guessing maybe ten or so years younger. He's still working and going to school for heaven's sake."

Gordon took his mother's hand and patted it. "We'll be leaving for home in a couple of hours. Promise me you'll stay out of trouble until we see you again at Thanksgiving."

"I promise."

"No more strangers for lunch and no jumping into any rivers." He laughed when she blushed.

Chapter Forty-four

She ran her thoughts on inviting Robert to Thanksgiving dinner by Jake who agreed wholeheartedly.

"If the man's been living on the streets for nearly a year, I'm sure he would appreciate a hearty meal with regular folks in a regular home."

"I don't know how regular we are. We seem like an unsettled lot at the moment with you just visiting, waiting for me to pack my bags for a vacation away, and Gordon and Gracie coming here to look for a new place to live."

"Maybe we shouldn't tell him you like to go swimming in the Ottawa River in October."

She gave him a poke in the arm. "I think I'll call him tomorrow. After that I'll invite my neighbours in for a drink so I can explain to them who Robert is and what he's been up to. They've been accusing me of not being myself lately and I think they believe the man has established an influence of some kind over me."

❣ ❣ ❣

Sarah and Jake spent the day before Thanksgiving preparing food and getting the silverware cleaned. Jake reminded her of the formal meal she had prepared the first time he had visited Ottawa. "It took you two days to get the food ready and a day to set up the dining room table. Then it took me three days to help you wash and store away again all your fancy china and stuff."

"I think you're exaggerating more than a little, but you're right. I like special occasions to be special. Gracie will be here to help me tomorrow. I want her to learn how to set a table properly."

"Didn't her momma do that?"

"Her mother had caterers do all that. All the food prep. All the table prep. All the cleanup after. The hardest work Gracie had to do was seat her little bum down in her chair and place her soiled napkin beside her plate when she was finished."

"She doesn't act like a child used to being treated like a princess."

"You're right." Sarah thought about it. "She is growing into a nice, polite young woman."

"Guess she inherited her Grandma Eisenboch's genes."

Before Sarah could respond, Gordon and Gracie came in the door.

"Where are your overnight bags?" Sarah watched as they came in empty handed.

"I guess you didn't get my message last night telling you that we had arrived and decided to stay in a hotel."

"No." Sarah glanced over and saw the red light blinking on her landline phone.

"We have a few appointments for apartment viewings today so we didn't want to get in your way coming and going. We just came from a nice place now that Gracie thinks might be *the* one." He looked around the kitchen and peeked into the dining room and saw the linen and china waiting. "Are you expecting the queen to show up?"

"Gordon, you know I like a nice table. I'm hoping Gracie will give me a hand tomorrow. You're not house shopping tomorrow, are you?"

"No. We'll come early so you can show her the ropes." He kissed his mother's forehead. "You do realize that anyone under sixty doesn't use china and sterling silver anymore? Gracie will probably have nothing in her kitchen or dining room that can't be loaded into a dishwasher or put into a microwave."

"At least she'll know what fork to use when she visits in a home that still practises fine dining."

Just then her doorbell rang and she learned that the flower arrangement for the dining room table had arrived. Gordon rolled his eyes and patted Jake on the shoulder. "You have my condolences, Jake. You'll be the unwitting victim of all this graciousness now." Then he popped some grapes into his mouth and smiled at his mother. "I hear most places are only using bamboo plates and grass tablecloths in Hawaii these days."

"At least their flowers will be fresh." She smiled.

♥♥♥

Late on the morning of Thanksgiving, the turkey was placed in the oven. A lasagna that had been prepared the day before was all set to be baked, and a glazed, decorated ham was waiting for the oven as well.

"Now I know why you have all these stoves in here. It seemed overmuch for one lady when I first saw your kitchen. Do you do all this again at Christmas time?"

"I do. Unless my family is invited elsewhere."

"Then what do you do?"

"I help cook the turkeys at a shelter downtown."

"Of course you do." Jake shook his head then planted a kiss on top of Sarah's head.

Gracie had stayed through the previous evening and they got the dining room table set. She was curious about this other man that her grandmother had invited for supper.

"But how did you meet him, Grandma?"

Sarah had hesitated telling her granddaughter about Bob portraying a homeless person. She was worried about influencing Sarah's impression about the man. She wanted the girl to see the person he was, not the person he had presented himself as.

"We ... uh ... met on the sidewalk outside. He was doing some research for a paper he's working on."

"And you just had a conversation?"

"Something like that. We kept running into each other and finally we became friends."

"Doesn't he have a family?"

"No." She had learned that he had been engaged at one time but that ended when he went overseas with the armed forces.

❦ ❦ ❦

It was Jake who opened the door for Robert when he arrived.

"You must be Sarah's friend, Robert." Jake extended his hand.

"Bob. I prefer Bob." He accepted Jake's hand and gave it a firm grip.

"I'm Jake. Sarah's friend visiting from Chicago."

Jake motioned for Bob to go ahead into the living room just as Gordon came into the room. The two men exchanged greetings and Gordon offered to get Bob something to drink.

"Your guest is here, Mom." Gordon motioned to the other room as he grabbed a beer from the fridge for Bob.

Sarah finished putting the vegetable bowl in the warmer and Gracie followed her.

Bob stood and extended his hand to Sarah. "Thank you for including me today." He handed her a small, gift-wrapped box.

Sarah thanked him and told everyone to sit down. She turned to introduce Gracie and found the girl staring at their guest.

"Dad, Mr. Archer has a dimple in his chin just like yours."

Everyone one turned to look at Bob then at Gordon.

Chapter Forty-five

When Gordie had been born, Gordon senior had looked proudly at the cleft in his son's chin and told Sarah that his father had one also. It was apparently a characteristic of generations of Hawkes males. Sarah recalled the conversation now, as she stared at the two men, slightly similar in appearance, standing in front of her.

Jake broke the moment by lifting his chin and pointing out that he also had one. Not as deep as the other two men but an indentation none the less for all to see.

"My daddy used to tell me it was the mark of a handsome man, made us look like Clark Gable."

"You won't hear me argue against that." Gordon laughed and the moment passed.

"Who's Clark Gable?" Gracie asked.

"Just about the handsomest man who ever filled a movie screen." Jake stuck his chin out and tilted his head as if posing for a picture.

Sarah opened the gift box and smiled when she found inside a small gold pin: a guardian angel with a rhinestone in her halo accompanied by a card with "Thank you from the book guy."

♥ ♥ ♥

The meal seemed to satisfy the palates of all at the table. The men found common ground enough to keep them talking. Gracie helped her grandmother serve each course and remove the plates after each. Jake winked at Sarah when the girl politely asked if he was through with his utensils before clearing the place in front of him to make room for the dessert.

Sarah watched as Bob removed the pecans she had placed on the top of the slice of banana cream pie placed in front of him. She had not put any on Gordon's plate knowing he was not partial to them.

"Are you allergic to nuts, Bob? I should have asked before putting them on your pie."

"No. I just prefer the pie without them, thank you. It's delicious by the way."

The goosebumps on her arms were back. So many similarities.

"Did you know that my grandma jumped into the rapids in the river last week?"

Bob looked at Gracie then at Sarah.

"You jumped in or you fell in?" His question was a mixture of concern and astonishment.

"She jumped in to save Jake." Gracie was beaming with pride. "We went white-water rafting and Jake fell in and Grandma thought he was drowning so she jumped in to save him."

Bob looked at Sarah with new admiration. "You went white-water rafting? In October?"

"It was not my idea, believe me." Sarah offered to get more coffee for everyone.

When she came back Gracie was regaling the story of the promise Jake made to her if she learned to play a new piece of music on the piano.

"I not only learned a new piece, but I learned one that Jake said was one of the hardest pieces to play."

"What one was that?" She had Bob's attention.

"The Entertainer." Her puffed-up chest displayed her pride.

"That is a difficult piece." Bob agreed.

"Do you play the piano?" Gracie asked.

"I do. My mother was very strict about my learning to play."

"Did you have to take lessons?"

"No piano lessons, no hockey. That was the deal."

"Wow, your mom must have been strict. Did your dad make you play too?"

"I never knew my dad. He ... died when I was young."

"Oh, that's too bad. I know how you must feel because my mom died last winter." Gracie looked at Gordon as she said it.

"I got by." Bob smiled at Gracie. "I understand I inherited some of my dad's traits so I feel like he's a part of me. I'll bet you have some of your mom in you too."

"Yeah. My mom was cool. She could be really strict too though. Just like yours. She wanted me to play the piano and be good in sports too. She was hoping I'd go to the same college she did and you have to have super good marks and be super athletic to get in there."

"What did your mom do before she died?"

"If you mean what kind of work, she didn't. She mostly just looked after me. Did your mother work?"

"Yes, she was a secretary."

"Cool."

Sarah was about to change the subject and hopefully lighten the mood a bit when Gracie asked, "Where was she a secretary?"

"She worked for a while for a man who was a vice-president in an engineering firm in Cornwall then she moved to Ottawa and worked for the government until she died."

"What engineering firm was that?" It was Gordon asking the question.

"It was sold in the mid-1980's, then closed completely in the '90s. St. Lawrence Engineering."

"I've heard of it. Mom, isn't that where my grandfather

worked?" He looked at Bob again. "Hey, maybe your mother knew him."

The goosebumps returned to Sarah's arms.

"I believe it might have been. Gracie, will you help me carry some of these dishes into the kitchen? And why don't you gentlemen go and make yourselves comfortable in the living room. We'll join you shortly."

"Thank you, Sarah, but if you don't think me rude, I'll leave now before I get too comfortable. I promised to help with the cleanup at the shelter this evening."

"Of course. Can I give you a doggy bag to take for your supper tomorrow?"

"I was hoping you would offer." He smiled.

Sarah packed some leftovers into plastic containers and Bob left, promising to be in touch again after her return from Hawaii. Gracie asked permission to go to Kelly's place to spend an hour with her before her and her dad's return to Montreal. She had to be back in school the next morning so they were going to make the two-hour trip home that evening.

When Gordon and Jake carried the last of the dishes into the kitchen, they found Sarah sobbing.

"Mom, what's wrong?"

"I ... I don't know, son. I am emotionally wrecked."

"Why? What brought this on?"

"Come and sit down." Sarah led the two men into the living room. "I have noticed a few things about Bob over time that sparked nervous reactions. I tried to pass them off as coincidences but after tonight, I'm afraid my suspicions might have some credence."

"Do you think he's a crook after all?" Gordon put an arm around his mother.

"No. I don't think that at all." She looked from Gordon to Jake and back to Gordon again.

"Do you want me to make myself scarce, darlin'?"

"No, Jake. It's okay." She put her hand on Gordon's. "I don't think Bob is a crook but I would like you to do me a favour, Gordon. I would like for you to have one of those DNA tests done."

"Why?"

"I think there's a good possibility that Robert Archer might be your uncle."

Chapter Forty-six

"My uncle? Come on, Mom. Just because he has a dimple in his chin? That's ridiculous."

Sarah could feel the tension in Gordon's tone.

"It's not ridiculous, Gordon." She reached for her son's hand. "There are too many similarities for it to be a coincidence. Or ridiculous."

"Wouldn't Dad have told you if he had a brother?"

"I don't think he knew. I don't think anyone knew except Bob's mother ... and your grandfather."

"What? You think Grandpa had a fling and no one knew about it? What about Grandma, wouldn't she have known?

"Maybe she did and didn't want to acknowledge it. Then again, maybe she didn't."

"A baby is a pretty hard thing to keep hidden. Bob said his dad was very generous. How could Grandpa financially keep two families fed and housed?"

"I don't know. I just have this eerie feeling you and he might have matching genes." She gave her son's hand a squeeze. "He was the recipient of the blood you donated. You both share a rare blood type for one thing."

Gordon's whole body stiffened. "Have you mentioned this to Bob?"

"Only about your being the blood donor. Gordie, this is why I would like you to have your DNA done. If I'm way out in left field then nothing more needs to be done or said."

"And if you're right …?"

"We'll cross that bridge when we come to it."

"How will we know unless he has his DNA done also. You can't just casually ask him over a cup of coffee to go have it done."

Gracie came in the door so they had to cut the conversation short.

"I'll figure it out. In the meantime, please have yours done."

❣ ❣ ❣

Sarah was glad she was leaving on vacation in a couple of days. There were so many thoughts running rampant in her mind, it was becoming increasingly difficult to keep them to herself. She didn't want to discuss anything with her friends until she knew for sure. She knew everyone would be certain it wasn't a coincidence that Bob literally showed up on her doorstep one night. They would automatically assume he knew who she was and that he was after her money. That it was all part of a well-orchestrated scheme to dupe her out of his share of her fortune. Her argument would be that he was not entitled to anything. Most of her money had come from Harold, not Gordon. As Gordon's brother, he wouldn't be considered an heir of his money either. Or would he? No. Gordon's money had been earned by Gordon, not inherited from his dad. She remembered Gordon's dad dying almost penniless even though he had been a corporate vice-president of a large company. No wonder. He had spent every cent he made keeping two families, not just one. Besides, Bob seemed to have done well for himself. He was well-educated. He had an excellent job with a reputable university. She didn't have just his word on that, she had looked him up. Pictures and all.

❣ ❣ ❣

What to pack was the question of the moment. She had

picked up new casual summer items at the end of summer. She mostly wore capris, T-shirts and long summer dresses during the hot humid days of Ottawa summers. Would that kind of attire be suitable for Hawaii?

"It's going to have to be. I am not going shopping."

"Who are you talking to?" Jake stopped at her bedroom door.

"The fashion gods." She closed the lid on her suitcase. "I hate shopping and I hate packing. That's what I love about Florida. My clothes are already there. I just have to bring a few replacements with me."

"Well, that's something I can't help you with, darlin'. I'm packing some golf shorts and shirts, a couple swim trunks, and a pair of nice pants to take you out for a fancy dinner a time or two. I figure I'll pick up some of those Hawaiian flowered shirts once I'm there so I don't look like a tourist."

Sarah laughed. "I'll bet the tourists are the only ones who wear those shirts."

"You're probably right." He gave her a peck on the cheek. "Shall I call Uber to pick us up in the morning?"

"Gerald said he'd drive us to the airport."

♥ ♥ ♥

Jake lived in a bungalow in one of the suburbs of Chicago. It had been built in the '80s, but he had maintained it well and it looked like he and his wife had renovated and updated the floor plan sometime in the not too distant past. There were pictures on a console table of Jake and her, another of their daughter's graduation, and another with their daughter, son-in-law and grandchildren. A perfect suburban family home for a perfect suburban family. Jake's wife had been tall, almost shoulder to shoulder with him.

"Jennifer was the star on her college basketball team back in the day." He picked up the family portrait and stared at it for a moment or two. "Denise is almost as tall as her mother. She preferred tennis to basketball though."

"Tennis is more a life-time sport, I would think. Something in which she can participate well into her old age."

"Yep. She was pretty good at it. Didn't go beyond state trials though. She wasn't as competitive as her mother."

"I can't imagine how hard it must be living half a world away from them."

"I'm thinking I might go there for a while sometime late winter or spring."

"Jake, don't just think about it. Do it. Your grandchildren surely would be happy to see you."

He stared at the picture. "Yes. I think spending so much time with your sweet granddaughter has made me miss them even more. I'll find out from Denise when would be a good time to plan it. Their summers are too hot so she'll probably suggest either spring or fall."

He rubbed his hands together. "Now what would you like me to grill for you on the barbecue?"

"Surprise me."

"I'll run to the supermarket up the road and see what they have that looks nice and juicy for grilling. You go outside and relax. I'll fix you a nice cold drink to enjoy while I'm gone."

♥♥♥

He came back to find her sound asleep in the hammock with her drink untouched, ice cubes melted by a warm October sun.

Chapter Forty-seven

Just as all the brochures had promised, the weather had been perfect the whole first week of their tropical paradise. There were short-lived, daily showers that never lasted long enough to dampen any of their sightseeing plans, either literally or figuratively. In a week they had seen everything there was to see on the Island of Oahu including the USS Arizona Memorial. Waikiki Beach lived up to all the hype and an evening dinner cruise gifted them with a sunset beyond belief.

Jake proved to be a great travel companion. He agreed readily to her choices of sightseeing adventures and was thoughtful of her in his own choices. They golfed. They swam. They rode the trolleys and enjoyed the food. After a fun-filled busy week, they boarded a small plane for Maui.

♥ ♥ ♥

They learned they were a little early in the season for whale watching but the golf courses were in excellent shape and that made them happy. The sightseeing was slightly different on this island too. There were rugged hiking trails from which they chose the beginner trails only. They kayaked along beaches and waterways. Mostly, they relaxed on the lanai and enjoyed the fresh breezes, mountain and ocean views.

"Ya know, darlin', I could get used to this I think." Jake was stretched out on a lounge in the shade, drink in hand.

"It's certainly not hard to take." Sarah was relaxing with a novel, embracing the warm fingers of breezes caressing her bare legs.

"Happy you came?"

"More than happy, Jake. I didn't know what I was missing by always zeroing in on Florida. Thank you for pulling me out of my comfort zone and getting me to experience another part of the world."

"These islands sure can take a person back to another point in time. An easier, gentler time. I can't imagine what's going on in the rest of the world right now, nor do I care. Does it even matter what day, month or year it is? It's always the same here — winter, summer, spring or fall."

Sarah glanced over at Jake as he lay with his eyes closed. He was such a gentle man. She wished she had his laid-back attitude. She took in his form. His hair was a silver-sandy mix with just enough curl to make it always look slightly dishevelled. His forearms were powerful for a man in his late sixties. He didn't have six-pack abs — more like a beer belly. The well-muscled calves came from his almost daily walks on the golf course. She knew that's how his arms maintained their strength also. His face had the weathered texture that came from daily sun on it but offset by a softness that cried out kindness. His forehead had a dividing line where his baseball cap protected the upper part from the sun. He wasn't handsome but he had a sexiness about him, especially when his eyes were closed and his thick eyelashes rested on his cheeks. Her friends were right. He was a catch.

"What are you thinking about?"

"I'm reading."

"I haven't heard you turn a page for quite a while."

"I'm reading you."

His eyes opened with a start. "Do you like what you're reading?"

Sarah laughed. "You know I do." She put her book down.

"Especially, when you're lying there feigning sleep and letting your muscles glisten in the sunshine."

"What can I say? I can't help it if I have a Clint Eastwood body."

"Clint Eastwood, is it? Too sinewy. I'm drawn to men with more meat on them." She looked at his belly and winked as she said it. "Besides he's much older than you."

"Glad to hear that." He sat up, sucked in his stomach and flexed his arm muscles. "How about I get you a fresh drink then I think we should get dressed for the luau tonight."

"I'll pass on the drink but you're right, I'd better start getting ready. It's going to take me a while to look like I belong on the arm of such a big, strong, handsome man. You just have to oil your body and put on a colourful shirt while I have to start with a pedicure and then ... Oh lord ... The time I'll need for my face and hair."

♥ ♥ ♥

It was the perfect evening for a luau. The sunset was even more spectacular than from the dinner cruise on Waikiki Beach. The roast pig done on a spit tasted like no pork Sarah had ever experienced. Perfection. The music and dancers were fantastically entertaining. While the drums were beating and the soft sounds of the ukuleles carried romantically across the night air, Sarah was more than content sitting in the arms of the man beside her. She had never felt more at peace. She glanced up at him and smiled. He kissed her temple in response.

"Happy darlin'?"

"I couldn't be more so." She caressed his cheek and brought her lips to his, lingering longer than usual.

Walking through the foyer of their hotel afterward, she felt life couldn't get any better than this.

"I'm going to remember this evening forever. It was the most magnificent, breathtaking, romantic date I have ever had.

Thank you for this fabulous last night, Jake."

She was about to put her arms around him and kiss him again right there on the spot when she heard someone gasp, followed by … "Mother?"

Chapter Forty-eight

"Emily? What are you doing here, darling?"

"I told you that Daniel and I were taking an October vacation. I'm sure I said we were coming to Hawaii."

"I don't think so. I would have remembered. It's wonderful to see you, Emily." She reached to embrace her daughter in a hug but the younger woman backed away. The action left Sarah embarrassed and emotionally undone.

Daniel reached for his mother-in-law and embraced her. Sarah had always had a good rapport with Emily's husband and he obviously felt Sarah's discomfort with his wife's reaction. Sarah turned to Jake and introduced her daughter and son-in-law. The two men shook hands.

"So you're my mother's latest?"

Sarah's back stiffened. Emily could be as angry as she wanted at her but Jake didn't deserve rudeness like this. Before she could respond to her daughter's sarcastic remark, Jake responded.

"Your mother and I have been friends for years. I don't know about latest but long time for sure. It's taken me all these years to convince Sarah I'm worthy of some bonus time away from Florida." He smiled at the younger woman. "It's nice to meet you, Emily. You too, Daniel. Why don't you join us in our suite for a nightcap? We're leaving on a morning flight so it will be the only chance to visit."

Emily hesitated but her husband acknowledged the invitation and said they could come in for a short while. They had arrived just that evening and it was already quite late for them because of the time change. He put his hand on Emily's back and gently nudged her to follow Jake and Sarah.

Jake mixed drinks and opened the large doors onto the lanai. They remained inside in the sitting room but could hear the night noises and feel the warm night breeze. Sarah was unsure how to open the conversation. She had hoped that someday Emily and Jake might meet but certainly not with the tension that weighed heavily among them in this moment.

"How long have you been here?" It was Daniel who broke the silence.

Sarah explained they had enjoyed a week on Oahu before spending this past week on Maui. "I can't believe how beautiful it is on the islands. It has taken me almost sixty-five years to get here but it won't take much coaxing to get me back."

Jake asked if this was their first trip. When Emily was unresponsive, Daniel told them it was their third time here. He reminded Sarah that the two had honeymooned in Honolulu then had come to Maui for their tenth anniversary.

"We prefer this island. It's a little more relaxing and scenic than Oahu." He glanced at his wife who was busy looking around the suite. "We like to snorkel and golf and this island has more of that to offer than any other."

"Too bad you didn't get here a few days earlier we could have made a foursome on the golf course." Jake was smiling at Daniel.

"Mom didn't say you were coming here, only that she planned on being away this month." Emily stopped her tour of the rooms and sat with her drink.

"Too bad. How long are you staying?"

Emily responded to Jake. "We're here for ten days." She looked at her mother. "I doubt that we'd have gone golfing anyway. Mother never did make time to do things with me even back home in Canada. Why start here and now?"

"It's never too late to make up for lost time." Sarah tried to sound stronger than she felt.

"You're wrong. It *is* too late."

"No. It definitely is not." Daniel's voice was stronger than Sarah had ever heard him use when talking to his wife. "This is the perfect time and the perfect place to make up."

Emily stood. "Daniel, not now. Not tonight. We'll talk about this when we're back home."

"Yes, now." He put an arm around his wife's shoulder. "I think it's time to tell your mother all the things you've wanted to say for a long, long time."

He lifted Emily's chin and forced her to look at him. "I don't think it's any coincidence you bumped into each in a hotel lobby thousands of miles from home. You are being given an opportunity. Don't mess it up."

She nodded at him almost indiscernibly.

Daniel turned to Jake. "Can we take our drinks out to the lanai?"

Jake nodded and motioned Daniel outside. They slid the door most of the way closed behind them.

Sarah and Emily stared awkwardly at each other for a few minutes before Emily set her glass down on one of the tables. She turned her back on her mother and crossed her arms. A few moments slid past before Sarah saw her daughter's shoulders shaking. She crossed the space between them and took Emily into her arms. A sob escaped Emily's throat so loud that it startled the men outside.

The two women hugged each other in a desperate attempt to erase any distance between them. Mother kissed daughter on her forehead then daughter buried her face in mother's shoulder and cried. And cried. The two men left the lanai and walked toward the beach.

♥ ♥ ♥

About forty-five minutes later, the men returned to find the two women sitting on the swing on the lanai, arms around each other in quiet conversation. When Emily saw them approach she pulled away from her mother and ran to her husband. She kissed him with so much love and gratitude that Sarah knew things would always be right between them. All of them.

Jake took the seat Emily had vacated on the swing and put his arm around Sarah. She placed her head on his shoulder and patted his chest then looked across at Daniel. "Thank you."

Chapter Forty-nine

They were well out over the Pacific Ocean before it really sank in that over forty years of reserve, actually downright coolness, distance and hurt, had dissolved in a matter of a half an hour. Emily had opened the floodgate once the tears started. Sarah had gone through outbursts from Emily before but usually it was a steady volume of accusations and hurtful references to her supposed neglect of her daughter. This time, it was more an appeal for understanding and Sarah listened and understood. She let her daughter get it all out of her system. The pleas for forgiveness on both parts were heartfelt and followed by tender gestures of the love that can only be shared between a mother and daughter.

After Emily and Daniel had left, Sarah explained to Jake what had just taken place. He was aware that the relationship between the two women was strained but had never realized how wide the chasm had been. Sarah's first thoughts were to stay another day or two and try to strengthen the newfound bond between her and her daughter but Jake suggested giving Emily the opportunity to collect herself and spend some quiet time with her husband. He reminded her that Daniel had been the one to bring it to a head. That he was the one responsible for Emily's facing up to her emotions and making peace with Sarah.

"He's the one she needs right now, darlin'. He took a giant and dangerous step in forcing her to face you. He must have known she was ready, otherwise I don't think he would have pressed her to speak up. He must have been absolutely certain it was something she deep down wanted. Let them have each other right now. She promised to call you when they get back to Canada and you'll have the rest of your life to show her how much you've always loved her."

His words had made sense. He and Daniel had known exactly what to do at the time. Two men who had met only minutes before had been on the same wavelength and had given the two women the time needed to come to grips with the love they felt and the years of inattention to it that had torn them apart.

She leaned on his arm now and caressed his hand that lay on her thigh. He kissed her temple and moved her head to nestle against his upper chest. He didn't speak. He was just there for her as always. She realized how much this man meant to her. This vacation had given her two things she had so badly needed in her life: the love and understanding of her daughter and the caring support of a man she certainly was unworthy of.

"You know all my secrets now. My life has been laid bare. I'm not the kind, charitable woman you thought I was. I drove my oldest child to a life of misery. Instead of giving her love, I neglected her in order to give her 'things'. I was too proud to ask for social assistance which would have enabled me to stay at home more with my child and give her the hugs and love that she desperately needed. I was too embarrassed by the fact that my husband had left me to think about the child who needed my love more than ever. It was all about me and my needs, my wants. I had to prove I could do it on my own, that I didn't need him. It took her husband to make me see that.

"It took Daniel, who understood his wife so well and loved her so much that he was willing to risk their marriage by demanding that she stand up to me and tell me exactly what she was feeling. Tell me what she needed. She could have walked right out of that room and left us both standing there but she didn't. He knew she wouldn't. He knew how broken her heart was and how badly it needed mending. He knew only I could heal it since it was me who had broken it."

"I think he also knew how much she loved you. That's what he based his decision on. I think he knew how much you loved her as well. Two women who love each other. Two women who had to be placed in a room together to kill the monster that was devouring both."

"You are such a wise man, Jakub Tatarek. One of the reasons I love you so much."

He stirred. "Did I just hear the word love?"

"Yes, but you know too much about me now. I'm either going to have to kill you or marry you." She stiffened in the seat. "Sorry. Wrong choice of words since I've already done both to two men before you."

"You meant that phrase in humour and I take it as such. What I will take seriously though is that you actually spoke of love and marriage in the same conversation."

Sarah sat up and turned to him. "Yes, I did, didn't I?"

She leaned over and kissed him softly on the mouth.

"Have I ever told you that you're the best kisser ever?"

Chapter Fifty

"What the hell, Mom! You go away and all hell breaks loose."

Sarah had checked her phone upon landing in O'Hare International Airport. She had turned it off before take-off in Hawaii and now saw there were several messages from Gordon to call him immediately.

"What is it, sweetheart? What's wrong?"

"Wrong? I don't know if wrong is the right word but some weird stuff sure has been happening."

"Like what?" She kind of expected what he was about to tell her.

"Did you already know that Bob had his DNA done a while back?"

"Yes."

"And you didn't say anything?"

"There was nothing really to say. He told me it had only disclosed a couple of very distant hits on his father's side but several on his mother's which he was already aware of. He had been disappointed that nothing showed up to identify his father. Why?"

"Well, he'll have a hit now. My results just came back and he and I have a close genetic connection."

Jake was by the carousel waiting for their luggage to slide out. Sarah was sorry it was in such a public setting that she was receiving this news. There were so many questions needing answers and the airport was not the place for this conversation.

"Does it tell you what the connection is? I've never seen results from those tests so I don't know what they look like."

"It looks like you may be right, Mom. Bob probably is my uncle."

Sarah saw Jake coming toward her with their luggage, waving for her to follow him to the taxi queue.

"Jake and I are just trying to flag a taxi to his place. Can I call you from there? That will give me time to digest this news. Is it something you can send me a picture or a pdf of for me to see?"

"I'll see how I can send it to you. Call me as soon as you can. I'm sure Bob will receive a notice of this match. When he does, we don't know what his reaction will be." Then as an afterthought, "Love you. Glad you got back safe and sound. I hear you met up with Emily. We have to talk about that too."

He closed the connection before Sarah had a chance to absorb that last piece of information. How did he know about Emily? *Emily must have called him.* She was standing staring at her phone when Jake called to her and pointed to a cab with the door open.

❦ ❦ ❦

When planning their itinerary, they had discussed her taking a connecting flight back to Ottawa while still at the airport but Jake's travel agent had informed them there would be a long delay between flights which would put her arriving home very late at night. That initiated her decision to stay at Jake's for a couple of days before going home. It had seemed like a good plan at the time.

❦ ❦ ❦

They were barely in the door when Sarah received a phone call from Bob letting her know that he had just received a notice from the ancestor search company he had ordered his DNA from telling him that he had a new match.

"Lo and behold the new match's name is one Gordon Hawkes! What in hell's name is going on, Sarah? Are you and your family checking me out? We need to talk. Soon."

"I'm in Chicago, Bob. I won't be home until the day after tomorrow. We landed just hours ago from Hawaii." She sat at the kitchen table and put her head in one hand. "Gordon called me a short while ago to tell me he received the same match notification. And yes, I did ask him to have a DNA test done. There were too many similarities between you and him for it to be coincidental. I thought if there was no match then no harm was done and that would be the end of it. I was not checking you out for any other reason than I believed you might be family and it would make me happy if you were."

"Why didn't you discuss this with me before doing it?"

"I can see now that I probably should have but hindsight is exactly that, hindsight. Can we talk about this when I get back home? I think you, Gordon and I have a lot of questions that need answers. From what I can gather on so little information, I think you and Gordon's father might have been brothers. That would make you my brother-in-law. Please try come to my place day after tomorrow to talk."

She explained the situation to Jake after he finished calling his favourite pizza delivery place.

"You had a strong hunch this was going to be the case, Sarah. You said that some of Bob's quirks reminded you of your late husband. How do you feel about him being part of your family now that it looks like he is?"

"I think I'm happier for Gordon than for myself. He was too young when his father died to remember much about him. I think it will be great for him to have a male relative, someone with his father's blood. Harry was a really good father to him in every respect but I think Gordie felt himself the lone male in a family of women once his stepdad passed away."

❣ ❣ ❣

Sarah's emotions were being pulled in every direction. So much had happened in the past twenty-four hours. It was a helluva lot to absorb: her daughter's acceptance and forgiveness; finding out that Bob was closely related to her son and that her husband had had a brother he knew nothing about; that the possibility was strong that her daughter had made contact with her brother after all these years; and the fact she had uttered the word "marry" in connection with Jake after vowing she would never, ever do that a fourth time.

Good lord, I feel like Zsa Zsa Gabor.

She was grateful that Jake didn't bring up, or push any further, their conversation on the plane. Good old Jake. It seemed he put everyone, her included, ahead of himself. He would have sensed she was too distraught, elated, nervous, and anxious about what the next few days were going to bring to put any added pressure on her about anything. It made her realize again what a good man he was and how lucky she was to have him in her life. *I'm going to do everything I can to make sure you stay, Jakub Tatarek.*

❣ ❣ ❣

She was surprised when Gordon met her at the airport — alone.

"Where's Gracie?"

"She's at Margaret and Clarke's."

"It's too bad you had to take her out of school."

"We'll talk about all of that when we get to your place." He worked his way out of the airport area and onto Bronson Avenue.

After carrying her luggage into her bedroom, he asked if he could make some tea for the two of them.

"Okay, Mom. Where do we start? With Bob or with Emily or

is there some other starting point I don't know about yet?"

Sarah was relieved to see the humour in his eyes and the shake of his head in disbelief.

"Maybe now is not the time to say that Jake and I have brought up the subject of getting married."

That brought a jolt of the head from Gordon followed by a boisterous bout of laughter. "What a week this has been. Mom, I don't think we'll ever top this one. I have more news also."

He stirred some sugar into his tea. "Gracie and I will be moving into our new condo on the top floor of this building. Hopefully by Christmas."

Tears were shimmering in Sarah's eyes. "All I can say is that from where I sit everything that's happening is good news. Magnificent news."

Gordon hesitated. "Is it, Mom?"

"In my eyes, yes."

"I was worried that you might think Gracie and my moving here, into your building, was a little invasive of your privacy."

"Son, you and Gracie could move right in here with me and I'd be happy." She motioned toward her living space.

Gordon squeezed her hand. "Now let's talk about Emily."

Sarah explained what had happened the few evenings before in Hawaii.

"So you say that Daniel was responsible for forcing Emily's hand ... and yours?"

"Yes. He took quite a chance confronting her like that. All I can guess is that they must have had conversations about this for him to be so sure she would respond positively."

"It was a long time coming, Mom, and I am so happy that it happened. Emily even hinted at seeing each other at Christmas time."

"Does she know you're moving into this building?"

"Yes. She commented it will make things easier for us all to be together if it works out."

The tears came then. "This has been my dream for so many years. I was afraid to hope it would ever come true."

"Well, now there's Jake and good old Uncle Bob to add to the equation. We may need to rent the banquet room to hold us all. I couldn't be more happy about you and Jake by the way. You know that Gracie and I both love the guy." He poured fresh tea into their cups and broke a cookie in half.

"Now, what about Bob, Mom?"

"I asked him to come here today. Have you spoken to him at all?"

"No. I wanted to wait for you."

"How do you feel about learning, in all probability, that you have an uncle? Besides Uncle Bruce of course."

Sarah's brother, two years her senior, had moved to Alberta many years before and they had virtually lost touch with each other.

"Bob seems like a nice guy. I really don't know what I feel. I guess I'll form an attachment as I get to know him. If I get to know him. Do you know how he feels?"

"He was upset when he called me. He thought we were checking up on him in the extreme. He felt we should have discussed it with him beforehand. I explained my thought was that there was no harm done if there was no connection but that I was very happy to find that there was. He's coming this evening and we'll talk about it. Will you and Gracie stay?"

"I have an appointment tomorrow with someone from the school she'll be attending. I also have some papers to sign at the lawyer's regarding our condo purchase. So, yes, we'll be here tonight. I can ask Margaret to keep her there for supper and an evening visit with Kelly if you like."

"Have you spoken to Margaret or any of them about what's been happening?"

"Not a word. I haven't even said anything to Gracie aside from our purchase of the condo upstairs. Poor kid, she's so excited and was upset when I told her not to tell anyone of our move until we've had a chance to discuss it with you."

Chapter Fifty-one

Sarah invited Bob to join her and Gordon for supper. When the doorbell rang it was Gordon who answered it and promptly gave Bob's hand a sturdy shake. The two men eyed each other warily before Sarah called out for them to join her in the dining room.

It was an awkward few moments while they exchanged greetings and niceties then Bob broke the tension. "I … I'm sorry I was so abrupt with you the other evening, Sarah. My surprise — shock really — at receiving that notice was no excuse for rudeness."

"I was equally surprised." Gordon smiled at Bob. "My first reaction was shock then came the realization that I may have met and conversed with my father's brother without even knowing one even existed."

"Then you can imagine *my* shock at finding out that I had a brother and a nephew. At least that's what the indications are."

Sarah put a hand on Bob's arm. "Not just a brother, but a wonderful, kind, loving man. I feel so bad that the two of you never got to meet each other."

"How old were you when he died?" Bob was looking intently at Gordon.

"Three years old. My memories of him are mostly my mother's and the photographs we have."

Sarah motioned to the food on the table. "Let's eat, then we can look at those photographs. Bob, you may see some of the similarities."

It was an emotional couple of hours. Sarah showed pictures to Bob of Gordon senior as a child and a teenager, then as a young man. She pointed out the same hair, the cleft in the chin, the angle the two men held their heads at times. The same slightly crooked smile.

"Would you like to see pictures of my father-in-law? Your father? I removed them from the album in case you weren't ready to see them."

Bob paused. Sarah could see he was uncertain.

"Another time maybe?"

"No. No, it's just that I've had my own image of my father all these years. One I had built up inside my head. It's crazy, but never having seen him, or even a picture of him, I'm ... I'm not sure what I'm feeling."

Sarah wrapped his shoulder with her arm. "I can put several of these in an envelope if you like and you can look at them when you are alone. I can't imagine how traumatic this must be."

"I'm ..." Bob turned to Gordon. "The DNA report was quite conclusive. I'd be a fool not to recognize that your father was my half-brother. It's ... I'm just having a hard time accepting that I have a family. I've been alone almost half of my fifty-five years — not answering to anyone, not having to consider anyone else's schedule or plans, not having to remember anyone's birthday ... or buy anyone a Christmas gift." He lowered his head to his hands and let his tears fall. Then he looked from Sarah to Gordon. "On the other hand, I've had no one ... no one ... to call family."

Gordon crouched in front of his newfound uncle and placed a hand on the man's tightly clenched fist. "I have to confess that I was distrustful of you at first. I warned my mother to keep her distance from you. I thought you were a scammer wanting to play a rich widow for a fool. Mom is such a good judge of character, I should have trusted her instincts. She felt a kinship to you from the very start. When she pointed out the similarities between you and me, I reluctantly agreed there were a few. I'm not surprised that our DNA is linked. It means a lot to me to learn that my dad's genes are alive and well in a previously unknown brother. I have no doubt that you're my uncle."

He stood and Bob stood with him. The two men embraced each other just as Gracie came in the door.

"Hi, Bob. I didn't know you were here. I would have come back sooner." Then she saw the tears in everyone's eyes. "What's going on? Did someone die?"

Her dad placed an arm around her shoulder. "No, Gracie. No one died. These are happy tears. We just learned that Bob is not just Bob. He's Uncle Bob. My dad's brother."

Gracie looked from one to the other in bewilderment then raised her eyebrows to her grandmother.

"Yes, it's true, sweetheart. Your dad and Bob are related. Isn't that wonderful news? You were right when you spotted a likeness between the two of them."

"So, does that make you my uncle too?"

"I guess technically I'm your great-uncle but Uncle Bob sounds just fine." He wiped his eyes. "More than fine."

Gracie reached out and placed her arms around her new uncle's chest.

Bob reached for the envelope containing pictures of his father and said, "I think it's time I looked at these."

♥ ♥ ♥

Bob had left, with Gracie making him promise to join them for Christmas. She had so many questions, Gordon said he'd have to answer them on their ride home the next day.

"I can't believe I have another uncle, even if it's a great-uncle."

♥ ♥ ♥

Sarah's head was spinning and her emotions were stretched to the limit by the time she pulled the sheets back on her bed. She made herself comfortable then dialed Jake's number.

"Hello, darlin'."

"Ah Jake, I needed to hear your sweet 'darlin'." She kissed the phone. "I have so much to talk to you about."

"I'm listening. I have some things to talk to you about too when you're done."

♥ ♥ ♥

The next afternoon she was sitting at Olivia's dining room table sharing tea and scones with her friends.

"These scones are delicious, Olivia. They simply melt in your mouth. You must give me your recipe." She lathered some strawberry jam on a piece and slipped it into her mouth.

"I didn't make them, Stella did."

"Enough about scones. Sarah, you have to tell us about your past two weeks."

They watched impatiently as Sarah put another piece of the tasty pastry in her mouth and blotted her lips.

"Where do you want me to start?" She smiled coyly at the faces of her friends and placed a finger on the side of her cheek, pondering …

"Hmm. Shall I start with telling you about my romantic, amazing two weeks in Hawaii? Or with the news that Gordon and Gracie just bought a condo in this very building and will be settled in here for Christmas? Or with the news that Emily and I have made amends with each other and she and her family will be joining us for Christmas? Or that Jake and I have decided to get married and honeymoon in Australia in the spring when we visit his daughter? Or … that DNA tests have proven that last winter's homeless man is my brother-in-law?"

Acknowledgments

As always, eternal gratitude to my talented book designer, friend and critic, Sherrill Wark, owner of Crowe Creations; with love to my family who always give me the utmost support; and to all my friends and acquaintances who provide me with inspiration and fodder for my stories.

About the Author

Born in Estevan, Saskatchewan, Phyllis was brought to Fort William (now Thunder Bay) as a toddler and grew up on the beautiful shores of Lake Superior. Now living in retirement near Ottawa, she continues to write and has become well-known for weaving gripping tales of romance and mystery featuring mostly places she has either lived or visited. The setting for all her novels is Canada, some with sojourns outside the country, and most of her books introduce fascinating characters who are fifty plus.

Sarah Eisenboch is the third novel in the *73 Windsor* series. Watch for a fourth sometime in 2023. Besides this series, Phyllis has five stand-alone romantic/suspense novels published and is currently working on another.

A complete background of her, her work and her books can be found on her website www.phyllisbohonis.com

Previously Published Novels

Fire in the Foothills
The Wilderness
Tomorrow's Promise
The Track
Never Marry a Farmer

<u>The 73 Windsor Series:</u>
Helen Whittaker
Margaret McFarland

CPSIA information can be obtained
at www.ICGtesting.com
Printed in the USA
LVHW081544100522
718377LV00035B/653

9 781999 437855